Mating Dance

Black Hills Wolves Book 50

By

Merryn Dexter

Copyright © 2016 by Merryn Dexter
ISBN: 978-1-68361-068-7
Cover art by Fiona Jayde

Published by
Decadent Publishing Company, LLC

Look for us online at:
www.decadentpublishing.com

~A Note from the Author~

It was a joy to return to the Black Hills and spend time with the Tao Pack again. When the opportunity arose to create a story for this special Matchmakers line, I jumped at the chance to revisit my beloved characters from A Mate's Healing Touch and A Mate's Redeeming Touch and introduce another member of the Burrows family.

In telling the story of Sander and Rory I wanted to write an "imperfect" romance, a story where things go wrong for the couple more often than they go right. I knew they would get a Happy Ever After (this is why I love to write romance!), I just hope they can both forgive me for leading them a merry dance along the way.

I would love to hear what you think about this 'Second Chance' romance. You can find me on Facebook and Twitter via the links below.
https://www.facebook.com/merryn.dexter
https://twitter.com/MerrynDexter

Alternatively, please email me - merryndexter@gmail.com .

Cheers!
Merryn

Dedication

To M. who is my perfect match.

Chapter One

Rain battered the windshield as Sander Burrows forced the beaten sedan too fast around the corner. The wipers were shot and the scrape of rubber against glass tortured his sensitive ears. Mickey Sullivan, his partner for the past two years, braced himself against the side window as he swigged the cold dregs of a cup of takeout coffee.

"Jesus, Lashes! We'll be no good to the kid if we end up in a fender bender."

Sander grunted in apology but didn't ease up on the gas. Mickey was right, but the details of the 911 call had turned his guts to acid. The first responders were ahead of them, but the system notified the taskforce of incidents in the neighborhood.

The "shots fired" report came from a block Sander knew well. He'd spent a lot of time there, both on and off duty, trying to get Nick Warren back on track. A good kid, like most he dealt with, who'd gone off the rails after his father died. Seeking a masculine role model in the wrong place, Nick had ended up a runner for a mid-level dealer. It wasn't just about the money it put in his pocket although Nick peddled a self-persuasive "it helps my mom and my sister" line of justification.

Sander had never argued with him on that point. Instead, he kept his message to the kid simple—be honest with himself. Being in the gang gave Nick a sense of purpose, of brotherhood—something Sander could appreciate, having been born into a pack. The key lay in getting the kid to recognize it took more courage to leave a group run by a bad leader than it did to stay.

Sander's brother Stefan had shown such courage, fleeing with his family when their mad alpha brought the pack into violent disarray. Guilt still gnawed Sander's conscience. Youthful wanderlust meant he hadn't been there to defend his niece from a madman's predations. The same guilt kept him away still in spite of his family's pleas to come home. They had returned to Los Lobos, the hometown he had left at twenty-two, feeling trapped. Magnum was dead and his son, Drew, continued to prove his worth as the alpha the Tao Pack needed.

Flashing blue and red lights blurred by the relentless downpour pulled Sander back to the present, and he slammed the car to the curb just before the taped-off cordon. He could hear Mickey panting in his wake as he showed his badge to the bored-looking patrolman. Hitting full speed, he ducked under the yellow tape and ran for the dreary, gray apartment building. A young kid, barely old enough to wear his dark-blue uniform stood nervously outside the door. Rain dripped off the brim of his hat, and he looked cold and scared as Sander stopped to show his ID again. *Scared could get him killed.* He paused.

"Take your hand off your holster, son," he growled. "Don't put your hand near that goddamn thing unless you intend to use it." Everything inside screamed at him to hurry, to get to the fourth-floor apartment and check on Nick, but the rookie spoke to every protective urge of a natural dominant.

"Go, Lashes. I'll sort this out." Mickey's out-of-breath words released the self-imposed trap, and Sander slammed through the door, hitting the first-floor landing with a leap no human could achieve. Fear over what he would discover made him reckless, and he clamped down, wresting control back from his wolf. The wolf viewed Nick and his family as theirs, a substitute for the family they couldn't be there to protect. Failure was a drumbeat, throbbing in time with the vein pulsing in his temple, echoing in every step as he climbed higher.

The fourth-floor corridor lay empty, the iron tang of blood hit his nose, and a keening sob stung his ears as he hurtled toward apartment 4G. The scarred white door stood ajar, a taunting reminder of all the times he'd passed through it in happier circumstances. He paused, bracing against the frame as he once again battled his wolf's aggression. His palm came away sticky, the smear of blood a precursor to the horror awaiting him.

The sight of the shabby brown carpet pulled him up short. Wet boot prints and other darker, viscous things marred the usually spotless surface. *Angie won't like the mess.* A ridiculous thought. Nick's house-proud mother had a damn sight more to worry about than dirty carpet. He scanned the room, his mind cataloguing the scene with the automatic detachment he'd developed after thirty-five years as a cop.

Good genes could explain away his youthful appearance for only so long then he moved on. Louisville was the third city he'd lived and worked in, fudging his age and records each time. He'd chosen it because he could drive an hour in any direction and be deep in a state forest or park. The guys from his precinct already teased him about his good looks, "Lashes" a reference to his pretty gray eyes framed by long dark eyelashes. He'd stayed too long this time; the desperate need to save kids like Nick had kept him lingering months past his set date to move.

His gaze skipped again and again to the little hand, so white against the dark blood soaking into the carpet beneath it. The keening voice of a mother in agony rose and fell before cutting off. Forcing his attention toward Angie, he stepped back under the force of the hatred flashing in her eyes. She rose on shaking legs, chest rising and falling in a rapid cadence as she tried to control her sobs enough to speak.

"Get out of my home." The waves of pain rolling across the room almost dropped him to his knees. Her ponytail hung askew, eyeliner smeared across her red cheeks like a ruin as she raised a shaking finger in his direction. "*You*. You did this!" The accusation knifed his heart, and he fought the urge to throw back his head and howl his anguish to the ceiling. The wolf bayed for blood and revenge, but the human part of Sander knew the triggerman would be another kid. Just like the one curled protectively around his sister's body. Another victim of the harsh reality of living in this part of town.

He raised his hand in supplication, reaching over the fallen bodies of Nick and his little sister as he appealed to the broken woman. For what, he didn't know. For forgiveness? *Fuck that, she has every right to her anger.* He dropped his hand to his side and forced himself to stare at the dead children before him. Whatever his intentions, he'd caused this.

With a single, silent nod, Sander turned and left the room, Angie's rising sobs battering his soul. The road to hell was paved with such things and he was bone-tired. Trudging down the corridor, he took out his cell phone and pressed a couple of keys. The smell of iron filled his nose, and he switched out the handset to his left. He studied the drying blood on his right palm as his last connection to sanity buzzed once, twice, three times before the laughing tones of his beloved sister-in-law pulled him back from the edge.

"Sander! Hello you gorgeous thing. You called just in time. Your little brother is being insufferable and I am all set to leave him." Her voice faded as if she turned away from the mouthpiece. "Stefan, it's your brother, and he's promised to whisk me away from this life of misery you subject me to."

The affection in her voice quite belied her words, and Sander smiled as he pictured Marjorie, red bobbed hair swinging, green eyes sparkling as she teased her mate. A smacking sound followed by a squeal and an outraged laugh narrowed the miles separating him from the truth he'd been ignoring for far too long.

"I need to come home, Margie." His voice, husky with unshed tears, betrayed his fraying emotions as he shoved his way out of the apartment building. On

5

the ground, he pushed past his partner, the kid, the flashing lights. All of it. His feet pounded on the slick pavement, duster raincoat billowing behind him as he ran hard. Ran toward what he needed—family, pack, the rolling majesty of the Black Hills.

Her gentle response offered a balm to his tattered soul. "We're here, Sander. We're here and we need you to come home, too."

***

Four weeks later

The month since his return to Los Lobos had passed in a blur of activity. Stefan and Marjorie threw him in at the deep end, keeping him so busy he fell asleep as soon as his head touched the pillow. It didn't stop the nightmares waking him, more often than not in a pool of sweat and regret, but it kept him from brooding too much during the day. It was impossible to keep a secret in a houseful of wolves. If the screams weren't enough, the sour reek of sweat on his sheets would be. The family chose not to mention them, and he chose to be grateful for their discretion.

Following the destruction of the barn, the former meeting place and source of so many painful memories, Drew had commissioned Stefan to construct a new function hall for the pack. Ross Luparell and his team helped draw the plans while Sander had been roped in as heavy labor. Good honest work, and it seemed important to demonstrate his commitment to assisting the pack in achieving its goals after so long away. A hard, brief conversation with Ryker, the pack enforcer, followed by a longer, no less tough one with Drew made it clear they expected everyone to contribute.

Recent events had tightened security, and no one rejoined the pack without being questioned. Sander's past among the humans as well as his familial connection helped to ease his return, but he needed to prove he could be trusted. Single males were subject to close scrutiny following the terrible events over the winter and without Stefan's support it would have been more of a challenge to fit in.

Rolling his shoulders to ease the ache in his back, Sander lifted the thick protective goggles onto his forehead and wiped the sweat from his brow with the bottom of his T-shirt. He paused to flip his middle finger at his nephew Caleb when he whistled in admiration.

"Nice tone, Unc! Don't let Hannah see or I'll have some competition."

Sander snorted and cuffed Caleb before slinging an arm around his shoulders. He was such a good man, a son any father would be proud of, and his utter adoration for his mate was returned wholeheartedly.

"Come on now, Caleb. You know there's only one female for me. We may have just met, but she owns me heart and soul. I'm looking forward to our hot date tonight." His nephew's laughing agreement almost covered the sound of rustling behind him. Sander turned, studying the bushes dotting the edge of the clearing, trying to locate the movement.

The area, even cleared of the charred ruins of the barn, still held a lingering scent of smoke. At least the fire had cleansed the spot of the overwhelming odors of blood, sweat, and pain. The rest of the crew described them as testament to the horrors of Magnum's cruelty. The land had been scoured and a fresh layer of dirt laid before the construction of the hall started. Wood shavings, sweat, and the myriad personal scents of the crew crisscrossed the ground.

He raised his head, taking a few steps away from the construction area to draw cleaner air into his lungs. *There.* Cranberries and vanilla. The scent tickled the back of his mind. He'd caught traces of it a time or two around the house. It tugged on some old memories he couldn't quite place.

There was no movement in the thick undergrowth, and, after a couple of minutes' study, he shrugged, making his way back to the worksite to pack away his equipment. Caleb waited by their truck, his gray eyes, the Burrows eyes, shining with excitement. Sander hurried to finish, not wanting to keep his nephew away from his mate and child any longer than necessary.

Tracking down the owner of the intriguing scent could wait for another day.

Chapter Two

R ory Hanson held her breath, lower lip clamped hard between her teeth to keep from making a noise as she peered through the tiny gap in the bushes. *You should have minded your own business, Rory. Should've just kept walking.* She'd been making her way to town to drop off a fresh batch of herbs to her new friend Bridie when curiosity got the better of her. The refurbishment and opening of the restaurant had been a blessing as it gave her another local customer to supplement her meager income. The fact the owner had become a rare friend was a surprising, but very welcome, offshoot.

Bridie and Will had moved to town following the return of Rory's best friend Marjorie Burrows and her family after ten years away from the pack. Their adopted daughter, Hannah, had recently mated with Marjorie's youngest son, Caleb. The return of her old friends and their extended family had drawn Rory back into the pack.

Marjorie thrived on the comings and goings of her family, but it was not a life Rory envied; well not *every* day. Like chalk and cheese, the two of them were total opposites—where Marjorie looked sleek and always immaculately turned out, Rory couldn't remember the last time she'd managed to get a comb through the mop of blonde curls rioting to her shoulders. It only got tangled again so she just washed it and left it. A bird's nest was the politest reference her best friend made to it. Bridie favored simple, practical outfits and struck a nice balance between the other two. She took Rory as she found her, another big plus in the friendship column. Her open, easy manner made her an instant favorite with many of the pack, even those wary about the influx of humans.

Not one for frills and frippery, Rory lived a simple life in one of the remote dwellings scattered around pack lands. Ryker had called her into town during the recent troubles and Marjorie had opened her beautiful home to her during those terrifying weeks when a murderer struck fear into the very heart of the pack. Although grateful for their generosity, the Burrows clan were a boisterous lot, and she had been relieved to return to the relative solitude of her simple one-room cabin.

Regardless of their surface differences, she and Marjorie had been friends for as long as anyone could remember. They'd met on the first day of school when Rory's grandmother escorted her to the door and left her to fend for herself. Gramma Hanson had been something of a wise woman, with a gift for herbalism she passed down to her only living relative, Rory. She'd learned her plant craft at Gramma's knee, and survived by foraging for herbs and flowers which she supplied to various businesses. Over the course of her long life, Gramma put together a huge book of plant pressings and recipes. Rory used it to provide traditional remedies to the healers of the pack, and it remained her most treasured possession.

Noise and laughter from the construction site had drawn her attention. Over lunch with Margie and Bridie, they'd discussed Stefan's new job. Drew had tasked him with building a new meeting place for the pack. Excited at seeing the progress, she'd diverted from her delivery to town, resulting in her current predicament. Her so-called best friend had failed to mention one salient fact over thick slices of cherry pie and coffee. Sander *Floofing* Burrows was back in town.

Dogsdamn that buster still looks hot enough to melt a glacier. Fifty-two years old and she still couldn't get past Gramma's abhorrence of cussing. The sting of her wooden spoon was still vivid, wielded when necessary until the day she died some ten years previous. As a result, Rory developed substitute curse words. They were now so ingrained it proved impossible to use anything else. She might have to try a bit harder when it came to the man who studied her hiding place.

Resisting the almost-desperate urge to run, she held her position. Pain gnawed her calf as the muscle spasmed in protest at being held rigid for too long. Heat warmed her cheeks as she glared at the source of her current discomfort. Her bitterness toward him shocked her. It wasn't as though she'd thought about him over the intervening years since *that day*. Rory squeezed her eyes shut and hoped the seat of her pants didn't start smoking because of the biggest dogsdamn lie she had ever told, even to herself.

Sander Burrows had hung the moon and stars for her from the day he'd pulled her pigtails when she was twelve.

She, Marjorie, and Stefan were the same age and had hung around together all the time. It had been clear to anyone with eyes Margie and Stefan would mate. Neither of them had so much as looked at anyone else since those first tentative steps beyond friendship. Five years their senior, it was a matter of fact that Sander was around and he had adopted the same big-brother role over all them. The feelings Rory held for him had never been sisterly. Scruffy and awkward, the ugly duckling to Margie's swan, she had kept her love for Sander tucked close to her heart. Every glance, every smile, and kind word had been examined and repeated over and over in her head. It was safe to love him in her dreams and so it had remained until the spring dance, not long after her seventeenth birthday. Marjorie had decided not only would Rory go to the dance, she would also need a date.

Shy and awkward, Rory had never been on a date. Never been kissed other than by Gramma and Marjorie. The adoption of a tomboy style had not been a conscious decision. She spent most of her free time helping Gramma forage, and Rory had never been one to draw attention to herself. Her right hand was disfigured, the missing ring and pinky fingers causing her to limp in her wolf form. The inevitable teasing and taunts had wounded her soft heart, so she had developed a "don't care" attitude as defense.

Caught in a hunter's trap when just a pup, she had gnawed off part of her paw to escape. The pain and panic from the trap and subsequent blood loss had caused her wolf to seize control and flee deep into the woods. By the time Gramma had summoned help for the search, too much time had passed for her eventual shift to human to heal the damage.

The sexy, *arrogant* man moved away, and Rory heaved a sigh of relief as she inched out from beneath the undergrowth. Her wild hair snagged on a branch, and she almost bit through her lip holding in the squeak of pain. Rubbing her abused scalp, she gathered her basket of herbs and returned to her original purpose.

***

Catching sight of the flapping green-and-white canvas, Rory smiled. She loved the restaurant. The bright striped awning added some much-needed color to Main Street. It sheltered a wooden boardwalk wide enough to hold a few metal tables and chairs. Will and Bridie understood some of the wolves did not enjoy crowded spaces, and the porch gave them a chance to eat in a comfortable space. Using her bottom to push the door open, Rory didn't see the matrons until it was too late. Pleading with the Fates to cut her a break, she forced a smile and ignored the roiling in her stomach as Miss Kathy snared her in a gimlet gaze. Miss Kathy's silver-streaked black hair spoke of age, although no one was stupid enough to ask exactly how old. No one who survived to tell the tale at any rate. Miss Kathy's cotton blouse was brightly patterned, and Rory winced as the elder studied her appearance with a critical snort.

"You been crawling through a hedge again, Aurora Jane?" Her voice carried across the room, drawing the attention of all the early dinner patrons toward the door. Startled at how close to the truth Miss Kathy was, Rory blushed. The older woman grinned knowingly. Although witches were nothing more than fairy tales, the younger members of the pack swore there was something spooky about the Native American wolf. Closing her eyes for a brief moment, Rory battled to hold her smile. Making a dash between the tables, she sought the relative safety of the kitchen area.

"Hold on there, Aurora!" Miss Lonnie called. Sister-in-law and partner in crime to Miss Kathy, the two were rarely seen apart. "Your arrival is serendipitous, my dear. We were just talking about you." Words to strike fear into the heart of the bravest wolf. Particularly when delivered by this smiling silver-haired woman. Knowing whatever they wanted would not improve by trying to delay, Rory changed course and presented herself to the four women. Miss Fern and Miss Claire completed the quartet. Best friends since school, the two were inseparable, their desire to meddle in the lives of the pack matched only by their love of baking.

Suppressing a shudder, Rory rested her basket on the edge of the table. These wily old women would pounce on the slightest hint of weakness. Baring her teeth in a gesture few would call a smile, she turned toward Miss Lonnie. Clad in a pair of gray coveralls, cuffs folded back neatly, it was clear Miss Lonnie had been "fixing" something again. She hoped for her friend's sake it was nothing from Bridie's kitchen. "Good day, Miss Lonnie. What can I help you with this afternoon?"

A bark of laughter from Miss Kathy showed they

were not taken in by her calm façade and Rory clasped her left hand over the damaged right one. A defensive gesture, a nervous tell she tried to avoid, but there were times, like now, when she couldn't control it. Miss Claire tutted at Miss Kathy who blew a raspberry and took a sip from the Bloody Mary in front of her.

"You must have heard about the new function hall being constructed." Miss Claire raised an eyebrow, and Rory squeezed her hands together to prevent lifting them to the heat striping her cheeks.

"Margie mentioned something about it," she muttered. Damn, she sounded like a sulky teenager, not a mature woman in her fifties.

"Well, my dear. We've been discussing all the wonderful things we can use the hall for, and you'll never guess what our first event is going to be!" Miss Claire bounced in her seat, voice rising with every word.

"Spring dance!" Miss Fern crowed from her seat in the corner. Miss Claire snapped her mouth shut as she spun to glare at her best friend. The two words were worse than anything Rory could have possibly imagined. Magnum's reign of terror had ensured the cancellation of any event unifying the pack, including innocent activities such as the dance. It had been a pack tradition from before Gramma's youth, a time for celebration and thanksgiving they'd survived the trials of winter. It had also been used to mark the transition from child to adult as school finished and teens began the roles defining their place in the pack.

The two women started to bicker, an old exchange about Miss Fern always stealing thunder and Miss Claire taking too long to get the point. Their distraction proved a boon, giving Rory a chance to compose herself a little. *Why would the matrons want to talk to me about my worst-ever nightmare?* Taking a deep breath, she rolled the tension from her neck as the familiar back and forth between the two women wound down. Plastering her fake smile back in place, she ignored the burning gaze of Miss Kathy from the other side of the table and spoke. "What exactly does any of this have to do with me?"

Miss Claire twitched as Miss Fern gave her a final dig in the ribs. She flapped her hand at the distraction, turning her body to angle more toward Rory, giving Miss Fern her back in the process. "You've always had such a beautiful eye, Aurora," she began.

"Not that anyone would know from the state of you, girl," Miss Kathy drawled.

Miss Claire shushed the interruption and tried again. "Oh ignore her, she's in a mood because Clyde's gone fishing again."

Miss Kathy snorted and rolled her eyes. "Sure, that's it. I'm pining for my mate," she muttered. Eyes narrowed, she turned her laser focus on Rory. "Such a shame you never found your mate, Aurora. Lots of wolves arriving in Los Lobos these days, old and new." The stress she put on the word *old* sent a shudder down Rory's spine. Miss Lonnie elbowed Miss Kathy hard, leaning forward over the table with a huge smile.

"Pay her no mind, honey, she's just teasing you. We're putting together a committee to help us plan the dance. Yours was the first name that came to mind to plan the decorations. As Claire so rightly pointed out, you have such a good eye. I always know when I see one of your arrangements." Miss Lonnie nodded to the wall above the table decorated with a dried wreath Rory had made as a gift for Bridie. Yellow roses of friendship, yarrow for good health, and azaleas for abundance were all interwoven around a ring of holly—the symbol of domestic happiness.

Unable to stay quiet any longer, Miss Claire butted in. "Yes. Exactly. With the knowledge Arabella handed down to you, you know more about plants and flowers than just about anyone. It wouldn't take up much of your time. Just a few hours a week. I'll be making cookies for the committee meetings." She winked and nodded, expectation bright in her eyes. Although Miss Claire was renowned for her outstanding cookies, it would take a damn sight more than a plate of them to get Rory within a million miles of the dance. Even the planning of it.

She held up her hand to stop the flow of words. "I'm sorry, ladies. I simply don't have the time to help you at the moment. I'm rushed off my feet supplying all the new businesses opening up. It takes too long to get in and out of town as it is." Her protests were met with a wall of indulgent smiles, as though she were some half-wit. *Time to try a different tack.* "Caress Galveston is marvelous with plants. I'm sure she'd be much more in touch with the younger elements of the pack. She'd be perfect for the job! I must get on now. Good afternoon!"

Ignoring the twinge of guilt at throwing the poor young wolf to the matrons, she grabbed her basket and sprinted for the safety of the kitchen. Swinging through the two-way door, she pressed her back against the wall next to it, clutching the basket protectively before her. "Floofing hell, that was a close one!" she gasped, fighting down the waves of panic clenching at her gut.

Raising her hand to her chest, Bridie huffed out a laugh. "Goodness, Rory. You blew in here like the hounds of hell are on your heels. Whatever is the matter?" She bustled to the sink, pouring a glass of water before crossing over and holding it out. She indicated toward the basket with her other hand, and Rory swapped one for the other, gulping gratefully at the cool liquid. Her throat felt drier than the bottom of a birdcage.

"I got cornered by the matrons," she whispered, and Bridie snorted.

"Say no more! They trapped poor Will earlier. I assume it's about the dance?" She rolled her eyes when Rory nodded. "We're doing the catering, apparently." She raised her voice in a fair imitation of Miss Fern's fluting tones. "Nothing fancy, won't take a minute."

Her voice darkened again. "Finger food for one hundred and twenty hungry wolves will take more than a bloody minute!"

Rory winced and waved her hands, trying to shush her friend. With their enhanced hearing, it was likely Bridie's rant would be heard by every wolf in the main dining area. The door swung open, and she braced, expecting an outraged matron to appear. Marjorie sailed in, and Rory sagged against the wall in relief. She fanned herself as her best friend kissed Bridie on the cheek. Marjorie looked immaculate as always. Her vibrant red hair cut into a sharp bob framed her heart-shaped face, not a lock out of place. Her camel-colored slacks were tucked into buttery-soft leather boots, topped with a cream blouse under a forest-green sweater which made her eyes glow.

Raising a hand to her own tangled mess, Rory tried to tuck the blonde strands behind her ear. Her fingers snagged, catching on something rough. Sighing at the hopelessness of it, she tugged a twig loose and studied it. It perfectly matched the bushes surrounding the construction site for the hall. Tucking it quickly into her jeans pocket, she offered her cheek for Marjorie's kiss before frowning and pulling back.

"You didn't tell me," she wailed. "You didn't tell me *he* was back in town!" Unable to stop the betraying quiver in her voice, she slid down the wall and came to rest on her heels as the realization hit her front and center.

Sander Burrows was home.

Chapter Three

Cradling the love of his life in his arms, Sander nodded his thanks to his niece's new mate as he held the door open for him to pass. A man of few words, most of them rude, Ven loved his mate, Caitlyn, with a hot, pure passion that softened his black eyes whenever they passed over her. Sander approved of their relationship. Caitlyn and Caleb had both made wonderful matches, one of which was directly responsible for the lightness in his own heart.

"Gruncle Sander?" The darling of his heart spoke, and he turned his full attention toward the little girl clinging to his neck. It had been love at first sight for both of them, and this precious child had been just about everything he needed to ease his battered soul.

"What is it, Messy Jessie?" She giggled at his special nickname for her. The first time they met, she'd been helping her mother, Hannah, bake cupcakes. Most of the chocolate mixture had ended up around Jessie's mouth, down her dress, up her arms. Everywhere but in the little paper sleeves where it belonged. It had also ended up all over him when a childish disregard for propriety, and the empathetic nature of her wolf, had flung her across the room to leap into his arms the moment he arrived. They had been inseparable ever since.

"Will you buy me a chocolate milk shake?" Jessie fluttered her lashes, the dimples in her cheeks flashing as she gave her best smile. Knowing full when he was being played by a master manipulator, he shook his head as he carried her into the busy room.

"Let's ask your momma what she says, okay?" He bent forward, lowering her to one of the chairs around the big table in the center of the restaurant before taking the one next to hers. Jessie glanced toward her mother who claimed the seat on the other side of her. Her pregnant belly bumped against the edge of the table, and she growled fit for any wolf, although latency kept hers buried deep inside. Kneeling on the seat, the little girl leaned toward Sander and whispered in his ear.

"Let's not ask her. She'll only say no." The sorrowful tone in her voice had him pulling back to study her. Moisture glinted in the corner of her eye and her lower lip quivered. His brother leaned across the table, capturing one of his granddaughter's curls between his fingers. He tugged gently to draw her limpid gaze from Sander, a mock frown creasing his forehead.

"Jessica...." The transformation was little short of miraculous as her expression flashed from abject sorrow to a cheeky grin. Holding his hands up in defeat, Sander rose toward the serving counter, brushing past the table of four older women as he did so. Cranberries and vanilla teased his nose, stopping him in his tracks. He inhaled, studying the women as they laughed over their evening cocktails. The scent didn't come from any of them, but a recent visitor to their table. The predatory grin from Miss Lonnie was enough to make him realize his mistake. It was never a good idea to put yourself in the matrons' path voluntarily.

"Ladies." He gave them a weak smile, edging away from their table and closer to the counter.

"Sander Burrows." A lesser wolf would've fled howling at Miss Claire's considering tone. Speculation gleamed in Miss Kathy's eye, turning his knees watery. The whump of the kitchen door captured his attention, and he heaved a sigh of relief as he spied his sister-in-law. Seizing on the excuse to escape the increasing scrutiny of the matrons, he hurried over, grabbing Marjorie in an enthusiastic hug.

"Margie, it's so great to see you!" *Go with it, sis. Please just go with it.*

"Oh, Sander! I was only gone a few minutes, is there a problem?" Marjorie laughed as she pulled back, although she kept a casual arm hooked around his waist. The sideways movement revealed the woman who had exited the kitchen behind her. His whole body came alive as the tangy-sweet scent that had teased him for days rolled through his senses like a heat wave. Blood swelled his cock, catching him by surprise. *At least I'm wearing a long jacket.*

Familiar aqua eyes peered up from beneath scowling brows as he studied the source of the alluring scent. Wild blonde curls snarled around her head, her curves emphasized by the simplicity of her clothing, a white T-shirt covered in dirt and boot-cut jeans. Tiny feet clad in practical sneakers added nothing to her five foot five height. A warm smile curled his lips as he recognized the little hellion beneath the womanly guise. "Hey, Rory, it's great to see you again."

The scowl didn't soften in response to his greeting. If anything, it deepened as the small woman reared back as though struck. "I'll see you later, Margie." The words were a direct snub, and he moved away from Marjorie, blocking Rory's path when she would have retreated.

"Hold up a minute, honey. I haven't been back in town five minutes. What can I possibly have done to upset you?" The restraining hand Marjorie placed on his arm should have warned him, but the fragrance that was uniquely Rory, fried his brain. The irrational anger she projected at him added a sharper undertone to her sweetness and rocked him on his heels. Rory Hanson was all grown up and Sander's wolf was *very* happy about it.

"What can you have possibly done to upset me? I see age hasn't lessened your arrogance, *honey*." The sarcasm dripping from her lips made him grin. Far from being deterred by it, Sander's natural dominance rose to the challenge of her glare. He wanted to scoop the scruffy little woman up and turn her over his knee until all her anger melted into sweet compliance. He stepped closer, deliberately putting himself within her personal space, knowing she would feel the heat boiling off his skin. He wanted her to know his scent, yearn for it the way he suddenly yearned for hers. He wanted to rub all up against her until forest green and sweet fruit intermingled.

Her scowl faltered to uncertainty, and she swayed toward him before retreating. Not liking the distance between them, he growled low, would've stepped close again had Marjorie not tightened her grip on his arm.

"I thought you had a hot date tonight?" Rory's cheeks flashed red as soon as she uttered the words, and he wondered where the hell the left field comment came from. She didn't wait for his response. Turning on her heel, she marched for the door.

He left it just long enough for her to think she was home free before he moved. Her hand froze on the door handle as he curled over her shoulder, pressing his weight against the palm he rested on the frame. She tugged ineffectually, her strength unable to compete with his, but he had to admire her effort. It didn't hurt any that her movements rubbed the luscious curves of her ass against his rock-hard cock.

Her breath came in little pants, the view over her shoulder of her ripe breasts heaving against the cotton of her shirt did nothing to calm his raging lust. Pressing his lips against the soft, pink shell of her ear, he whispered so his words wouldn't carry beyond them. "I'll only have a hot date tonight if you agree to take me home with you, *honey.*"

Arousal bloomed in her scent before it was stifled in the waves of distress emanating from her. The sudden change dampened his ardor. He stepped back, breaking their intimate connection. She didn't waste the opportunity. Tugging the door open, she was gone in a flash. Enjoying the view of her curvy behind for a few moments more, Sander grinned before closing the door.

The hunt was on. His wolf howled in approval, fur rubbing hard against the inside of his skin. Deciding their prey could wait for now, he released the sexual tension knotting his shoulders and turned back to join his family. The decision to return to Los Lobos was proving to be a good one.

Movement to his right caught his eye, and satisfaction shifted to dismay as he watched Miss Kathy beckoning him with one finger. Unable to avoid the irresistible tractor beam of the matrons' full attention, he forced a smile as he returned to their table. With what could only be described as a purr of satisfaction, Miss Lonnie reached across to pat his hand. "We have a job for you, Sander...."

***

It could have been a lot worse, he mused a week later as the truck bounced along the rutted path between the trees. "Path" gave the thinner section of undergrowth too much credit, and he was grateful for the loan of the four-wheel drive from his brother. The truck lurched as the offside front wheel hit a hidden pothole, and he gritted his teeth to avoid biting through his tongue. He rounded the corner. The sun burst through the thick canopy, revealing a small-but-sturdy cabin across a wide clearing. Tapping the brakes, Sander stopped the truck to stare in wonder at the vibrant display greeting him. Flowers of all types and colors flowed across the open area, a beautiful carpet. His heart lifted in simple joy at the sight of it. Succulents covered the roof of the cabin, a clever combination of drainage, insulation, and decoration. Hanging baskets swung from the overhang, bright balls of pansies, petunias, and geraniums trailing variegated ivy skirts.

The cabin door opened, framing Rory as she raised a hand to shield her eyes. Her stance slipped from curious to closed off. He slid from the truck and adopted a casual pose, resting against the side of the hood. Tucking his hands in the front pocket of his oldest jeans, the denim bleached almost white with age, he bided his time. Planning his strategy on the long drive out, he had decided a combination of relaxed friendship interspersed with intense moments would be the best way to lure his feisty little quarry. The combination of her scent and the giveaway comment about his "hot date" made it clear Rory had been spying on him at the construction site. An enlightening conversation with Marjorie had filled in the rest of the blanks. Too dumb to consider the consequences of his actions, he'd given in to the wanderlust gnawing at him from his late teens onward. Throwing his clothes into a duffle, he'd stuck a note on his bed and hit the road, completely forgetting he'd agreed to act as escort for Rory at the Spring Dance all those years ago.

His failure to show, combined with a hand-me-down unfashionable dress had left her the butt of the kind of cruelty only a group of teens was capable of. In spite of her tough exterior, he knew she was as soft as marshmallow on the inside, and guilt over his role in her humiliation bloomed bright. What had been nothing to him had clearly been everything to her. Time to make amends. His wolf was captivated and the man intrigued at the possibilities hiding beneath the flannel shirt and the scruffy hair. He wanted to take her to bed and watch her bloom like the flowers she so obviously loved. He kept his distance, not wanting to invade her territory more than he already had. Maintaining control over her environment would be important to such an independent wolf, and it would be an abuse of trust to use his superior dominance against her. So he waited. With a growl of frustration, she threw up her hands, stomped down the steps of the cabin and across the clearing.

"What the floof are you doing here?" she snapped.

"I'm your ride." Sander waggled his eyebrows and gave her a comic leer. Stifling a grin as her cheeks flushed at the double meaning in his words, he pulled open the passenger door and swept into a low bow. "Your chariot, m'lady."

"I'm not going anywhere with you, askhole!" Placing her hands on her hips only served to mold the flannel shirt closer, emphasizing her hourglass curves. He stayed in position, bent over, one arm folded across his waist, the other angled up and behind his back. Turning his gray eyes up to hers, he flashed another grin.

"Miss Lonnie explained your disappointment at not being able to make it into town for the dance meetings and asked if I would help you out. It's the least I can do for a fellow committee member." Her jaw dropped so far open, he feared she would dislocate it. Straightening, he gestured to the open door of the truck. "It doesn't pay to keep the matrons waiting."

Her gaping mouth snapped shut as she stared from him to the truck and back again. If memory served, it took some doing to shock Rory Hanson into silence, but apparently he'd achieved it. "The meeting starts at three and it's already past two thirty."

She didn't move, just continued to stare at him. Moving closer, he took her arm and guided her toward the vehicle. She climbed in without protest, turning to look at him through the open window. He pressed the door closed. Her plump lower lip glistened, inviting a wolf with an inclination to nibble on it before drawing it between his lips. And he was very inclined.

He forced himself to move back. Brushing the front of the truck in his haste to join her in the confines of the vehicle, he climbed into his seat. She turned her head to study him, as he snapped his seat belt on and started the engine. "I didn't agree to this. I didn't agree to any of this," she whispered. Her tone of defeat hurt his heart, and he tried to lighten the mood.

"It's the matrons. They're like the Borg." He wondered if she would get the joke, his time living amongst the humans had left him with an addiction to certain TV shows like *Star Trek*. He didn't remember a television from the few visits he'd made up to the cabin when they were kids though. Thankfully, the stupid joke did the trick, and her shuttered expression lightened as she mimicked his action and fixed her belt.

"Resistance is futile." She giggled, giving him a brief considering look through her lashes. She folded her hands in her lap. The movement drew his eyes to the scars on her right hand, to the tiny stumps of her missing digits. They had always been a part of her. Although some saw it as a weakness, Rory included, to him it was a symbol of her strong will to survive.

She tucked the three remaining fingers deeper under her left hand, and he bit back a growl. Turning his attention away from her, he backed the truck out of the clearing. Once Rory was his mate, he would make damn sure she never felt awkward or embarrassed about anything to do with herself.

Mate? Golden wolf eyes flashed as he flicked a glance at the rearview mirror. Her cranberry-and-vanilla scent warmed the interior of the cab, curling around his senses, settling into the deepest recesses of his being.

So be it.

Chapter Four

The scent of pine trees in winter filled her nose. Rory fought the urge to twist her head and bury her nose in the crook of his neck. The collar of the red-and-navy-striped polo shirt he wore was folded down, the buttons open, revealing an expanse of golden-brown skin. The brown curls she had always loved were just starting to show as his severe haircut grew out. Those same gray eyes, bracketed now by soft laughter lines, deepened to wet slate when she laughed at his joke. Gathering the shreds of her long-held resentment closer, she withdrew from the warmth she saw shining there.

It was too late for him to show an interest in her now. *Is it?* The wolf inside whispered and she shushed it sternly. That little traitor had always been keen to bare her throat to the dominant wolf looming large in every aspect of Sander's persona. She caught his eyes resting on her scars and automatically tucked the lame hand from sight. Hating feeling so exposed under his scrutiny, she turned toward the side window, watching the tree line as they bounced down the rough track toward town. The silence between them stretched as he steered carefully along the rutted path. He seemed content, concentrating on the path ahead, but the hairs on the back of her neck rose every time his eyes flicked in her direction.

Desperate to break the tension, she spoke. "So what have you been roped into doing for the dance?" She'd already conceded to handling the decorations. The matrons had outflanked her. By providing what seemed to be a perfectly reasonable solution to her transportation issues, they had backed her into a corner. If she made a fuss about Sander coming to fetch her, it would only draw more attention. They would ask why she didn't want to be around him. The last thing she needed was them thinking she had any feelings toward him.

"Ryker and his team are busy with the increased patrols so they've asked me to plan the security arrangements. I'm happy to do it as it will give me an opportunity to study the changes around town since I left." A lot had changed in the years he'd been away. Thriving homes had been abandoned to the elements by families fleeing persecution. Shops and stores stood empty, although recent arrivals were making inroads into reviving a number of businesses. New homes had sprung up, too, as Ross and his team worked hard to provide shelter for the influx of new arrivals. The recent spate of fires had destroyed more than just the barn as well.

"How will you fit that in around the construction work at the hall?" She shifted in her seat, studying the hard lines of his strong frame as he steered the truck down the hill.

"Oh I'm just grunt labor there. Stefan wanted to

keep me busy, and I was happy to lend a hand. I'll still pull shifts when he needs me, but there are plenty of skilled carpenters around who are better placed than me to do the technical stuff." A haunted look filled his eyes, and a deep frown marred his brow. His scent changed, an acrid thread marring the cool, clean fragrance. "I used to be a cop, but there's not much call for that here."

She nodded in understanding. Pack worked differently than the human world. The enforcer was in charge of protection, and he appointed his own team of trusted dominants and scouts. It would take time for a returnee like Sander to prove himself, to gain enough trust for one of those roles.

"I don't know what my purpose is anymore, Rory. I needed to come home, but now I'm here...." Pain and uncertainty filled his voice, unlike anything she remembered of the brash young man he'd been. So many years had passed, and he was different now. His face had lost its boyish softness, all hard planes and angles. His body had filled out, thickened through the shoulders, giving solidity to him.

Thinking about his body, she flashed back to the feel of him pressing up against her the previous evening. The solid, reassuring weight plastered over her back, the nudge of his cock against her ass. She closed her eyes as a rush of arousal arrowed into her belly, making it clench. She jabbed the button on the armrest to lower her window, the blast of cool air good against her flaming cheeks. A soft growl rose next to her and she squeezed her eyes shut. She hadn't been swift enough to clear the change in her scent from the confined space.

He braked hard, the sudden movement bumping

her against the side of the cab. She kept her eyes screwed shut. If she concentrated hard enough, perhaps she could teleport like some of the characters in her favorite books could do. A soft metallic click, a whisper of cotton, and warm breath bathed her neck. He was right there, filling up her space again, stealing the oxygen from her lungs. Her wolf whimpered, betraying their interest, and she knew he was close enough to hear her heart thunder in her chest. Frozen in place like a rabbit mesmerized in the presence of a predator, she waited. And waited. Nothing stirred in the cab other than the tangle of hair covering her neck as his steady breath tickled it against her skin. Anticipation built. She wanted to squirm at the tingle rising between her thighs.

"Look at me." Although soft, his tone brooked no resistance, and she flicked open one lid to peer at him. Gold shone in his eyes, the wolf studying his prey. He blinked and the gold washed back to dark gray. The force of passion she read there was more intense than even his wolf gaze. His tongue slicked across his lower lip. She watched in fascination as it slid lazily back and forth before disappearing again. "You and me, Rory." His words were a claim of possession, a declaration of intent.

"No," she whispered, her voice shaky.

"Yes." A statement of absolute fact. If she'd fancied herself in love with him as a girl, this new version of Sander had the ability to devour her heart in a single bite. She fumbled for the release handle. Flinging the door open, she made a bid for freedom. Unlike him, though, she had forgotten about her safety belt and the mechanism arrested her flight, pinning her back against the seat. Panic fluttered beneath her breastbone as she scrabbled for the lock, rising sharply as he grasped her damaged hand and held it firm in his grip. Reaching across her with his other hand, he closed her door, trapping her between the cool metal and the wicked heat of his body.

Those slate-gray eyes never left hers as he raised her hand to his lips, tracing the scars with soft kisses. His gentle movements spoke of a well of tenderness she was terrified to tap. "I won't hurt you, honey." Sincerity shone in his eyes. He pressed a kiss in the center of her palm before placing her hand in her lap. Her fingers curled, trying to capture and hold onto the promise he'd placed there. She wanted to believe. She wanted so much to believe all her childish hopes and fantasies had come to life at last.

Opening her mouth to acquiesce, to reach for this magical gift he offered, the ghosts of the past took advantage of her vulnerability. Harsh laughter and taunts rippled down the years, whispering in her mind words of rejection and mockery. He edged closer, his lips an inch from hers as those old insecurities took control. "You already did," she whispered. Her wolf whined as he pulled back, as though her words dealt him a physical blow.

He didn't speak, just calmly put his seat belt back on and steered the car onto the path. She regretted the words almost as soon as she said them. They were those of the sad, rejected girl not the woman she was now. Unfortunately, since her wolf had fixated on him so young, she had little-to-no experience with relationships. No one else had piqued her interest, and she had withdrawn further from the pack when Gramma had passed, not long after Marjorie and Stefan fled Los Lobos with their family.

The last few miles jolted past in a cloud of disappointment and regret, but she had neither the courage nor the experience to reach across the divide she'd created. The atmosphere was stifling, and she sighed with relief when the truck pulled up outside The Den. There were a couple of other cars parked outside, and Rory made sure to unclip her belt this time before she leapt from the cab. Her dash for the door of the bar was in vain, however. Sander's long legs ate up the ground behind her, and she found herself once again pinned between his body and a door.

His big hand lifted the hair from her nape and warm, surprisingly soft lips brushed the lightest of kisses against her sensitive skin. Goose bumps prickled all over her body as he growled in her ear. "I'll only let you push me away for so long, honey, and then there will be a reckoning between us." Threat or promise, she wasn't sure, the shudder racing through her not caused by fear alone.

As though the intimate moment had never happened, he stepped back and pulled the door open. Smiling broadly, he gestured for her to enter the bar. Keeping her eyes downcast, she shot past him, drawing a relieved breath when she saw several people hovering around a couple of tables which had been dragged together in the center of the room.

The voices of the matrons rose, drawing her attention to the hapless young man who was the current source of their consternation. Paul's body language was defensive as he alternately nodded, shook his head, and shrugged in response to their barrage of questions. Transformed by his recent mating, the barman no longer cowered in fear but still looked uncomfortable. His ability to communicate in sign language had come to light, and several members of the pack were taking lessons in ASL. His hands were hampered by a tray filled with glasses and soft drinks, ruling out any chance of proper communication. Feeling sorry for the omega and keen for an excuse to put some distance between herself and Sander, she hurried over to the bar.

Nudging between Miss Fern and Miss Claire, she caught Paul's eye. He gave Rory a sweetly grateful smile as she relieved him of the burden. Swinging around, she used the tray to nudge the ladies back, creating enough space for Paul to make a break for the kitchen. Sensing the four women bearing down on her as she moved toward the table, she quickened her steps. Grimacing at Sander, she rolled her eyes, indicating she needed his assistance with the unwanted entourage. He smirked at her exaggerated expressions. Folding his arms over his broad chest, he remained lounging in the chair he occupied. *Buster!*

She snarled silently, banging the tray onto the table before turning on the spot to face the music. Miss Fern, looking sassy in a powder-blue tracksuit accented with chunky turquoise accessories at her wrists and ears, gave her a beaming smile. She tucked her arm through Rory's, steering her away from the table, chattering a mile a minute. "Aurora, darling. So very good of you to join us! I remembered what good friends you and Sander were, and you looked so disappointed at missing out on the committee. Bless his heart, he jumped at the chance to chauffeur you around."

Rory whipped her head around, glaring over her

shoulder at Sander as the matron led her inexorably toward the door. He wiggled one finger at her in a mock wave before he paled as Miss Kathy plonked down in the seat next to him. *Serves you right!* Her attention returned to the door as a shaft of bright sunlight caused her to squint. Miss Claire held the door open with her back, both hands rummaging in the big pocket of her apron. The practical garment, hand sewn like most of her clothing, was a riot of orange and red poppies. The ever-present amber teardrop around her neck swung gently as she dug around, muttering to herself. She followed behind them, still digging as they headed toward Miss Fern's old, but impeccably kept, compact. The apron pocket clearly occupied a different dimensional space. Various items were withdrawn and tucked back in, until, with a crow of triumph, Miss Claire brandished a wide-toothed comb and a length of ribbon.

Trapped against the side of the car, Rory had no choice but to take the plastic-wrapped tray of cakes and sweets handed to her by Miss Fern. Miss Claire advanced with the comb, dragging it through the tangled bangs covering Rory's forehead, making her squeal in protest. A sharp tug at the back of her head had her trying to turn toward the new source of torture.

"Oh, hush yourself," Miss Claire admonished, tying the ribbon around Rory's head. The bright-blue ribbon pulled her hair away from her face. Miss Fern gave the back a few more hard brushes, bringing tears to Rory's eyes. She patted Rory on the cheek, nodding with satisfaction. "Much better, dear. You have such beautiful eyes, but how would anyone notice them hidden under all this hair?"

"I don't want anyone to notice my eyes, Miss Claire. Nor any other part of me, for that matter." She growled. They wore matching grins, more like Cheshire cats than wolves. Brushing past them, she stomped back toward the bar. Her childish fit of pique gave way to practicality. She still had her hands full with the tray of sweets, forcing her to wait by the door for one of the women to open it. Miss Fern rubbed her arm, a surreptitious gesture of kindness as she ushered her back inside.

Most of the places around the table were occupied as she placed the tray onto it and sidled around to the empty chair next to Paul. The omega gifted her another of his sweet smiles, jotting a quick note on the notepad he held. *Thank you.*

Lowering her voice to sub-vocal, she whispered back, "You're welcome. Always safety in numbers." A snicker came from the other side of Paul. Sander rested his forearms on the table. Everything in his body language indicated he gave all his attention to Miss Lonnie, who still huffed and complained, but his head cocked just enough she could tell he'd heard her comment.

Miss Kathy drained her glass of soda, banging it down like a gavel as she let rip a belch of such magnitude it must have been dragged up from her boots. "What?" she snapped at the gawking group before turning her attention toward Lonnie. "Put a damn sock in it. So your favorite cuddly bear isn't around, so what?"

Lonnie bristled and tutted at her friend's uncouth behavior. "Gee should be here," she grumbled, not willing to let her point go. Her eyes fixed once again on Paul, and he smiled weakly, holding up the pad and pen before hunching over it to show he was ready to take notes. With a sniff and one final tut, Miss Lonnie started the meeting, describing their aims for the party.

Rory leaned closer to Paul, half an ear on the matrons as they talked over each other. "Where's Gee?" she whispered, aware Sander shifted closer on Paul's other side.

He arranged a meeting with Drew. Said there was no point being here when he knows they'll get exactly what they want.

Rory stifled a grin as she pictured the big bear grumbling about being railroaded by the matrons. A sharp cough drew her eyes as Sander tried to cover a bark of laughter. Paul smiled silently between them as he made another note.

Besides, he's scared half to death of Miss Lonnie. She pays him a lot of attention whenever she comes to the bar. Something about Gee asking her on a date when they were young.

Eyes as round as saucers over the juicy tidbit, Rory risked another glance at Sander. His hand rested companionably on the young omega's shoulder, a huge grin transforming him from handsome to downright gorgeous. He looked so light and carefree, the years rolled back before her. Gone were the shadows and lines of the past thirty-five years. Here was *her* Sander—brash, fun loving, and generous with his time. Offering friendship to all members of the pack regardless of their dominance.

Thrum, thrum, thrum. Her pulse throbbed in her ears as she studied the man she had loved for most all of her life. His grin softened, the humor melting to a stronger, richer emotion. Paul tapped his pen softly on his pad. Sliding lower in his seat, he surreptitiously tried to escape his unexpected position of third wheel.

"Aurora? Aurora Jane!" Miss Lonnie rapped her knuckles on the table, startling Rory from her reverie.

"I'm sorry?" She turned toward the elder, the stars in her eyes shattering when she realized everyone around the table stared at her.

"We were talking about the decorations, dear," Miss Fern interjected gently. "Lonnie wanted to know if you had any thoughts on the design, a theme perhaps?"

Theme? Seriously? As of an hour ago, Rory had been ensconced in her nice, peaceful little cabin, believing she had successfully ducked the committee, and now they expected her to have a theme? "Umm, theme, theme, theme." She rubbed her damp palms on her jean-clad thighs, desperate to gather her scattered wits. "I thought I would open it up to suggestions. Do a little canvassing around town, see what the consensus is. Also, umm, until I have the dimensions of the hall, it's hard to know what I'm working with, how big it is." With a concerted effort, she forced her mouth shut against the stream of inanity.

"I'm sure that's something Sander can help you with, dear," Miss Lonnie said with a wicked smile as she turned her attention to the dark-haired wolf. "You'll be happy to show Aurora how big it is, won't you, Sander?" Turning in his seat, Sander took his sweet time as he studied her. His slow, lazy regard sent such a rush of blood to her cheeks, it made Rory light-headed.

"Miss Lonnie, I can't think of anything I'd like to

do more," he drawled.

Hunkering down in her seat, Rory prayed for the ground to open up and swallow her whole. With a soft sigh, Paul reached beneath the table and gave the back of her hand a sympathetic pat.

It didn't help. Nothing would help ever again.

Chapter Five

The conversation he had planned with Rory on the drive home didn't happen. She'd left the table at the end of the meeting and headed on back toward the bathrooms. Impatience got the better of him after ten minutes of hanging around, and he asked Paul to check on her. When the young omega returned with a neatly folded bundle of clothes in his hands, he knew the time had come to admit defeat. Rory had shifted and run. Disappointing, as he'd planned on a few kisses playing an integral role in the conversation. It would keep. For now.

Her clothing still sat on the passenger seat of his truck a week later. A lingering scent of cranberries and vanilla perfumed the cab, simultaneously soothing and rousing his wolf. The beast pressed hard for the hunt, and the man was close to breaking, but the pack seemed determined to put obstacles in his way. Sander had persuaded his brother to loan him a spare copy of the blueprints for the hall. He'd been trying to find time to pay Rory a visit and court her where there was no chance of interruption, no matter how well intentioned.

The matchmaking efforts of the matrons hadn't escaped his attention. They probably thought they were being clever in creating scenarios to push him and Rory together, and he had no complaints. As long as it didn't cause too many problems. Miss Lonnie was as subtle as a sledgehammer with her outrageous comments. Miss Claire's and Miss Fern's mini makeover had amused him as much as it irritated Rory. They didn't understand he was already sold on her just the way she was. He liked the edge of wildness about her, the independent streak she'd had to develop, living so isolated from the pack.

Drew had summoned him the day after the committee meeting to outline the role he wanted Sander to undertake within the pack. The request was bittersweet. Although it spoke to the deeply protective nature of Sander's wolf, it also served to remind him how badly he'd failed the last teen he'd tried to help. He also risked using his attraction to Rory as a way to avoid dealing with the recent past. It didn't invalidate his feelings for her, but he'd never been a coward. He needed to be the best possible version of himself he could muster to be worthy of his quarry. His desire for her would just have to wait, hence his wolf's restlessness.

Some of the older teens in the pack were gaining a reputation for unruly behavior. There had been some unpleasant instances of bullying, with groups of young men preying on those they deemed weaker or vulnerable. Although an understandable consequence of the turmoil within the pack, the time had come to stamp-out to such behavior. They'd been witness to too much cruelty when only children and were struggling to adjust to the changes Drew demanded of them. Ryker had too much on his plate already, protecting the pack. Add in his mate's pregnancy and he had little time and no tolerance for the escapades of a few young punks. His role as enforcer was often misunderstood. He'd been the ultimate bogeyman during Magnum's reign, and having the pack fear him had been a tool to distance himself from others. When the binding ties of a blood oath could force you to kill another at a madman's whim, it proved almost impossible to forge relationships.

Recent revelations had proven just how dedicated Ryker was to protecting the pack, even at the cost of his reputation. Many of those who'd disappeared were sent to safety, not killed as most had assumed. Ryker's mate, Saja, had begun helping with the efforts to trace the lost members of the pack and they were drifting home. Fear of the Enforcer was slowly turning to respect.

Drew had decreed Sander's experience made him the ideal candidate to run herd on the wayward youth. He'd asked him to design a program of activities and training which would instill discipline and a sense of responsibility, as well as helping the youngsters find a productive place among the pack. Sander knew from experience boredom and lack of attention were fertile breeding grounds for mischief, and his first suggestion had been greeted with enthusiasm by the alpha. It would require some alteration to the plans for the hall complex, nothing too major, but a couple of proposed meeting rooms would be sacrificed to create a youth club for the older teens and young adults in transition. Sander planned to make them responsible for the furnishing and decoration of the facility. He'd agreed on a budget with Drew, but the kids would have to decide between them what equipment they wanted. Having a safe place for them was the priority as well as giving them a sense of control over their environment.

He'd discussed the plan with his brother over dinner the previous night and been surprised, but delighted when Ven had volunteered to help him with the group. His niece's mate could be a prickly bastard until you got to know him. Ven had suffered terrible abuse as a young boy and his surly exterior provided a barrier against further hurts. Through the tender love of his mate, he had learned to shed the resentment and bitterness of his broken childhood. He would make a great role model for the boys, someone not too far removed from their age who wouldn't take any shit. Stefan and Marjorie had offered suggestions of others who might be interested in helping out with talks and mentoring. They'd also discussed suitable work placements for those who showed an aptitude. Stefan had agreed to offer an apprenticeship with his construction firm, and Ven had offered shifts at the gas station as a way for the teens to earn a little money. With excitement for the project building, he was ready to make the next move.

Knocking on the door of the schoolhouse, he was greeted with a bright smile from Adrie Scarlett, the head teacher. She had a tough job providing a suitable education program covering the spectrum of ages, particularly in such a small environment, and he admired her efforts. When he'd spoken to her a couple of days before, there had been a hint of relief in her voice. Student numbers were growing, and it would take some pressure off to have him bear some of the responsibility for the older children.

"Mr. Burrows, it's nice to finally meet you. Jessie has told us so much about you." The petite brown-haired woman smiled with real warmth as she ushered him in through the door.

"Sander, please."

"Sander, then, but you must call me Adrie. I can't tell you how excited I am about the potential for the program. My mate, Ravage, runs the gym in town and he's volunteered a couple of free training sessions a week if it would fit in with your plans?"

He nodded enthusiastically. "That would be fantastic. If it's going to work, it needs to be a pack-wide effort. We have to demonstrate how much we value this generation. Giving them secure role models is vital, and in as many different environments as possible. The dominants need a positive outlet for their aggression, but I also want to make space in the program for the others. A healthy pack needs artists as much as it needs protectors." He took a breath and laughed. "Sorry, my head is so full of ideas, I'm at risk of steamrolling everyone I meet!"

"Not at all! We've had some great success with our gardening program with all the children. Caress has done a wonderful job with it. She's been working closely with the teens so I'm sure she will have some valuable input." Adrie led him to the section of the schoolhouse partitioned off for the older children. The chatter died down as she entered and addressed the class. "This is Sander Burrows. He's rejoined the pack and will be running a new youth program here in Los Lobos. Please give him your full attention." A light pat in his arm and she was gone, leaving him facing a variety of expressions from openly interested to downright hostile.

Time to do my thing.

The discussion with the teens went better than expected, the girls generally more willing to put forward ideas than the boys. He made a mental note of who hadn't spoken as they would be his priority for one-to-one chats to ensure everyone's voice was heard. A young man at the back of the room had spent more time staring out of the window than anything. A study in boredom. Sander was pretty certain he had heard every word though.

He'd been the first to leave the room, and Sander had kept an eye on his direction. After speaking to everyone who stayed behind and fixing a time to review the plans for the club, he strolled around the back of the schoolhouse. His wolf perked up at the sight of a familiar, and thoroughly delicious, ass sticking up in the air as two women bent over one of the planting areas. Running into Rory was an unexpected pleasure, but he resisted his wolf's urging to pounce, drifting instead toward the teen who sat apart, partially hidden between the trees.

"Daniel?" He'd asked one of the other kids his name. The boy looked startled then wary at his approach.

"I'm not doing anything wrong," Daniel muttered, dropping the sketchbook he had next to him. The boy fiddled with a stray thread on his shirt, refusing to make eye contact.

"I'm not here to get on your case. I just wanted to know what you thought about the program." Sander slid down against one of the trees until he sat, legs crossed at the ankles. He watched the older and younger woman working in harmony in the garden. He didn't say anything else. The kid was skittish, and he didn't want him to feel compelled to respond to a more dominant adult.

"It's okay, if you like that sort of thing." A wistful note threaded beneath the belligerent response. Sander kept his body language relaxed, enjoying the view of his future mate's curvy butt wiggling around as she dug in the dirt. A soft growl rumbled in his chest as she leaned forward, stretching the denim tight. Her head whipped around, and she started at the sight of him. He blew her a kiss then laughed in delight when she sniffed in disgust before pointedly turning her back to him. He winked at her companion, Caress, who studied him with interest before leaning in to whisper something to Rory.

"I don't think she likes you," the boy scoffed then ducked his head as though expecting a blow. The wolf inside Sander didn't like the obvious sign of fear, not at all. *Young are to be nurtured, protected.*

"She's crazy about me, kid. Just playing hard to get." He glanced to his left, catching Daniel's eye to flash him a rueful grin. "Well that's what I'm hoping anyway. I'm a stubborn bastard. So's my wolf. We'll win her over with our irresistible charm." He waggled his eyebrows at the boy, pleased when he got a little smile in response. Hoping the ice had been broken enough, he gestured casually to the pad beside Daniel. "You like to draw, huh?"

The change in topic caught the kid off guard. He placed a protective hand over the top of the pad and shrugged. "I guess." Sander let the silence stretch, this time keeping his focus on the boy. Patience was a skill he had grown into, and there was nothing more pressing on his time than the desire to get Daniel to open up to him. A few more minutes passed before the boy muttered, "There are better things I could be doing."

The soft words hurt his heart. Someone with influence had apparently said those words to Daniel often enough for him to believe them. Sander possessed little in the way of artistic skills himself, but had always admired the talent in others. "Can I take a look?" The boy's hand on the sketch pad convulsed, and he feared he'd pushed too far, too fast. He held his breath, only relaxing when the boy shrugged as though it was no big deal and handed the pad to him. The tension in his body belied his attitude as he tugged over and over at the thread on his shirt.

The trust this child placed in him was a gift he would need to handle with infinite care. Placing the pad across his knees, he opened the cover and gasped. A charcoal leaf filled the first sheet, every vein and line shown in intricate detail. He flipped the page to find a side-on study of Adrie Scarlett. Page after page of exquisite images delighted him. Daniel had a remarkable talent with an eye for detail.

He waited to speak until he'd looked at every single drawing, paying due homage. "Have you shown these to anyone else?" Daniel shook his head, staring at his knees as though they were the most fascinating thing ever. "Do you take commissions?" The question shocked the boy, his brown eyes huge as he gaped at Sander. The idea someone would not just appreciate but covet one of his drawings had obviously never occurred to him.

"It's my sister-in-law's birthday in a few weeks.

Do you think if I got you some photos to work from, you could put something together for me?" The hope in Daniel's eyes broke Sander's heart. Before he could pursue the subject further, the boy glanced at his watch, and grabbed the sketch pad. The change in his scent, the reek of worry, had Sander's wolf's hackles up.

"I've gotta go. I can't be late." Daniel disappeared, scrambling through the undergrowth in his hurry.

Sander rose, unbuttoning his shirt as he approached the two women. Tugging his keys from his pocket, he tossed them toward Rory as he continued to strip. "Take the truck home. I'll be there later." Without pausing for an answer, he shucked his pants and boxers, leaving them in a pile at her feet.

Running for the trees, he dropped to his knees, answering the call of his wolf who clamored to get out. He let the shift come, the bright, fresh pain a joy in itself. After so many years of being fettered by life among the humans, it was a relief to be able to shift at will. Gray fur rippled as his limbs twisted, bones reshaping into his other self. Throwing his head back, the wolf bayed his challenge to the winds. They would hunt well today. First the source of Daniel's anxiety and then their mate.

Catching the sour taint threading the boy's natural scent, the wolf loped through the trees. It felt good to run, good to stretch his muscles again. His senses came alive as he slid through the undergrowth. The loamy smell of crushed plants underfoot created a backdrop for all the other notes. The sudden blast of mindless fear as a rabbit fled at his approach proved a momentary distraction before he pulled his wolf back on point. The boy's scent lay fresh and clear over everything, and he made sure to keep some distance, tracking upwind to keep from being noticed.

Crossing a wide, flattened area, he became confused by a tangled rush of scents. The pack had passed through here on a recent run, and the wolf wanted to roll in the power and fraternity of pack and family. He lost the scent he chased in the midst of so many others. Muzzle to the ground, he tracked back and forth, seeking the boy. The snap of a twig revealed his target, and he reluctantly abandoned the dazzling rainbow trail. The light changed overhead as the canopy thinned and the wolf slowed his pace. Hunkering low behind a fallen trunk, he watched the boy enter a cluster of houses.

The buildings were in various states of repair, a couple tumbledown, others neglected but showing signs of occupancy. One stood alone at the back of the group, worn and tired, but the surrounding area kept neat. Daniel headed straight for the wooden stairs, dashing up as the door swung open. A harassed-looking woman with a pair of toddlers clinging to her legs shook her head as the boy ducked his.

His foot scuffed on the bare planks of the little porch as the woman snapped, "Where were you? You know I can't afford to be late. Daydreaming, no doubt?" She snatched the sketchbook from under his arm, waving it under his nose as proof of her last words. Daniel didn't speak, instead crouching to gather the two little boys into his arms, lifting their weight easily. The woman continued to berate him, stepping aside to allow him to pass into the house. The door closed behind them, muffling her words, but Sander could tell they continued to flow.

He held position, calling on all of his patience and experience. Rushing in when the situation wasn't clear might prove a recipe for disaster, a lesson man and wolf had learned the hard way. It didn't take long before the door opened again. The woman emerged, tugging her coat over her shoulders as she rattled off instructions over her shoulder. He could just make out the shadow of Daniel's form, shoulders slumped, head hanging in a pose stinking of submission and defeat.

Sander gave the woman time to clear the area before shuffling back on his haunches, making sure the trees fully covered him before rising from his crouch. Shaking himself vigorously, the wolf scented the air before loping off toward the east. Signs of civilization thinned as his paws ate up the ground.

The hunt was on again, and this time he was determined he would find a more satisfying outcome.

Chapter Six

R ory paced the short distance between her bed and the kitchen area, the path taking her around the small dining table which marked the center of the cabin. The fragrance of dried herbs and flowers hanging from the exposed rafters filled the room although the heady lavender and lemon balm did little to calm her fraying nerves. The stack of clothing sat on the table, taunting her with images of Sander's sleekly muscled ass as he strode away from her earlier. She'd seen plenty of naked men before, Sander included. Wolves were pretty laid-back about nudity as few shifters had the ability to shift in their fully clothed state.

She turned another circuit of the room, refusing to check the hands on the old clock ticking quietly above her bed. They were unlikely to have moved since the last time she checked them, or the time before. Throwing up her hands in frustration, she grabbed the offending items from the table and marched from the cabin. *Should have left them in his truck in the first place.* Taking care not to squash any of her beloved plants, she wove a path across the clearing. The sun hung low on the horizon, painting the sky in a blaze of pinks and oranges. Undergrowth rustled close by her, and an impressive gray wolf stepped into the opening about six feet from her position. Golden eyes catching the fading rays of the sun, the wolf turned his head and studied her.

Wintergreen filled her senses, making the wolf inside her rub up against her skin. He was magnificent in both forms. The urge to shift, to press her muzzle into the deep fur at his throat and draw on his scent until she was drunk on it, almost overwhelming. The wolf padded closer, rubbing against her thigh in greeting, and she dropped her hand to the soft fur on the top of his head. He turned his head, nipping playfully at her fingers before stepping back a few paces. The wolf lowered his head, body rippling as the shift started. Fur melted away, surprising her with the ease of his shift. Sander knelt at her feet, shaking from the aftereffects. She didn't touch him; too much sensation for the newly shifted could be very uncomfortable. He looked up, brown curls plastered to his forehead by the sweat of his exertion. Heat burned in those familiar gray eyes, sparking a ripple of response low in her belly.

Dropping the clothing she hugged to her chest, Rory spun on her heel and made a dash for the cabin. A deep growl rolled across the clearing as he pursued her. *I've really got to stop giving him reasons to chase me.* Hot flesh bracketed her, pressing her hard against the unforgiving wood of the door. *Or maybe not,* whispered her wolf. A soft whine escaped her throat before she could swallow it down.

"What is it with you and doors, Sander Burrows?" She gasped as he pressed a thick thigh between her legs. Arms circling her waist, he tugged her back to rest against his chest. The hard muscle of his leg pressed the seam of her jeans close, rubbing the heavy material against her clit. Her resistance melted, as he scooped the hair away from her nape and nibbled at her sensitive pulse point. Liquid heat gushed from her core, and an approving rumble rose in his chest. "You smell so good, honey. So. Fucking. Good." Hot hands slid beneath her shirt, clasping her breasts, teasing her nipples into tight, aching points. She couldn't think straight as his tongue laved the side of her neck. Her focus zeroed down to those three points, and she braced her hands on the door, grinding her sex against his thigh to seek relief.

"Good girl. That's my beautiful, sexy girl. Do you want to come, honey?" he whispered in her ear, and she whined in response. "Unbutton your pants for me, Rory. Slide them down nice and slow." The pressure from his thigh disappeared, and she cried out at the loss of friction, scrabbling frantically at the fastening on her jeans. His grip on her chest shifted as he tugged the cups down until her breasts spilled out, the underwire in her bra holding them up for his touch. The zipper finally came free, and she shoved at the denim, kicking until her pants fell to her ankles, her practical white panties pooling on top of them. Cool air hit her ass, and she shivered, but it didn't stop her from tugging the T-shirt over her head. Sharp teeth grazed her neck and he pinched her nipples at the same time, the dual shocks arrowing to her core.

"My hands are full, Rory," he murmured. "You'll have to help me out." She paused, uncertain as to what he asked her, afraid she would do something wrong and betray her inexperience. He soon filled in the blanks. "Touch yourself, honey. Finger that hot little pussy of yours; show me what you like. I want your cream flowing when I fuck you with my tongue."

She dropped her hand hesitantly, cheeks flaming at the thought of masturbating in front of him. His thick erection nudged her ass, excitement and fear warring within her at the alien feel of it. "Do it for me," he panted, resting his chin on her shoulder, giving him line of sight down the front of her body. "I've dreamed about this, Rory. Dreamed about you coming apart in my arms."

The need to come was a hollow ache between her thighs, and she gasped in relief as she glanced her fingers over her clit. Pressing farther back, she was shocked at the slickness as she dipped just inside her pussy, dragging the moisture back to tease the bundle of nerves throbbing in time with her pulse. She knew exactly what she needed to do to come, the act as familiar as breathing after all these years. Pressing hard, she stroked herself rapidly.

"Yes, honey. That's it. You look so sexy. Does it feel good, darling? So beautiful, so hot." The litany of encouragement fell from his lips as sensation built to a level she had rarely felt. Getting herself off was mostly a stress reliever, a way to relax when sleep wouldn't come. She'd had no idea being intimate with another person would be this intense. And it wasn't just anyone.

It was him.

Past hurts faded in the reality of his touch. He was here. Now. And he wanted her.

"Sander." She gasped his name, faltering at the sensations threatening to overwhelm her. Releasing one of her breasts, he responded to the uncertain question in her voice, gliding his hand down the front of her belly until his fingers curled over hers, increasing the pressure on her throbbing clit.

"I've got you, Rory. I'm right here with you. Let it go, honey. It's okay." His soft assurance, the tenderness in his tone provided the perfect contrast to the riot of need inside. Clinging to the promise of safety, she gave herself over to the primal demands of her body. Her knees buckled as the strongest orgasm of her life ripped her apart. He braced her with ease, leaning back to take the limp weight of her body. Stars burst behind her tightly closed eyes, her breath sawing in and out of her lungs. He petted her, stroking her skin as he eased her back to awareness.

Reality came in a series of physical messages. The stretch in her throat where she'd thrown her head back against his shoulder. The press of his arm across her chest as he held her tightly against him. Wet heat on her fingers where they tangled with his at the juncture of her thighs. A throbbing pulse against her ass, his cock hard and ready to thrust inside her body. She catalogued them all as her wolf surged forward. *Ours. Take him, claim him. Mate.*

The wolf had no time for foolish emotion and doubt. She knew what she wanted, what was best for herself and her hesitant human half. Had it been up to the wolf, they would have made their feelings known years ago. Too much time had been wasted. The demands of her other half combined with her needs, the lonely, rejected girl so desperate for love.

Rory rolled her hips and the head of his cock slid between her thighs, gliding through the wetness coating her sex. Sander groaned against her ear, hot breath teasing her skin. His grip tightened, pressing their entwined fingers against her clit. A shudder of pleasure rippled down her spine, and he rubbed against her, seeking entry.

"Can you bend forward for me, honey?" He unlinked their hands, gripping her waist to shift her position even as he spoke, and she yielded to his guiding touch. She braced both hands against the door, her knees still shaky. Her weaker right hand didn't have sufficient strength to support her as he adjusted her to the angle he needed.

Pressure built against the entrance to her pussy as he aligned himself, and she tried to relax. Everyone said there was some pain the first time, and she clenched her teeth as the tip of his cock stretched her open. The burn in her swollen tissues brought tears to her eyes. He stopped moving. "Relax for me, Rory. You're a lot tighter than I expected, and I don't want to hurt you." His fingers flexed against her hips, sweat dripping from his brow onto her back.

What the heck does he think I'm trying to do? Exasperation battled with pain as she willed the contracted muscles at the entrance to her body to release. It wasn't like this in the romance novels she read. A pause, a quick thrust, white pain fading quickly to pleasure—that had been her expectation. Not this fiery invasion that felt as though he was tearing her apart. He pulled back, the tip of his cock slipping out. She gasped in relief. His forehead lowered to rest against her spine, and he sounded as though he struggled to get his breathing under control. "The thought of any other man touching you makes me crazy, but I have to ask, has it been a while since you had sex?" She could hear the wolf in his growled words. Squeezing her eyes shut, embarrassment and frustration warred with his right to know.

"It's fine, really. Try again, it…I heard…they say it's always painful the first time. Just do it." She pressed back again, seeking contact. His grip tightened, stilling her movements.

"Just do it?" The growl was gone, replaced by incredulity. Dammit, she was no good at this. The sexy words rolling so easily from his lips were a struggle for her. Trying to recall some of the seductive phrasing from her favorite stories, she wriggled her ass against him.

"Take me, Sander. Take me and make me yours." His lack of response made her panic, and she hunted desperately for the right words to get him back in the mood. "Fill me with your love rocket and ride me to the stars!" *Really?* Her wolf snorted in disgust, and Rory gave a mental apology.

The loss of his body heat when he stepped back combined with the vulnerability of her position, and sheer embarrassment to flip all her defensive switches. She straightened up, turning to place her back against the door, arms crossed to shield her body. He stood on the edge of the narrow porch, hands loose at his sides, a deep frown hooding his beautiful gray eyes.

"You're a virgin?" The tenderness in his voice translated to pity in her confused mind, and she lashed out.

"I waited thirty-five years for you! Thirty. Five. Years. Because my wolf decided you were the one. It's not my fault. I'm trying my best here!" Her voice wobbled as tears threatened to spill. Fumbling for the handle behind her, she whispered desperately. "It's not my fault."

He reached for her, but she evaded his hand. Stumbling back into the cabin, she shut him out, falling on her butt as the clothing around her ankles tripped her up. With a sob, she slid the bottom bolt home just as he pounded against the wood. Sprawled in the dark, she tried to catch her breath, the full horror of their failed coupling whirling through her mind.

"Rory! Dammit, honey, open up! We need to talk about this, please!"

"Go home!" Struggling to her knees, she turned the key to further secure the door. She tugged at the laces on her boots until she could kick them free, dragging the offending jeans from her legs. The bruise on her butt was nothing compared to the one on her ego, but it served to compound her humiliation. Grabbing a fleece blanket from the bed, she wrapped it around her shoulders before lowering gingerly to perch on the edge.

Disappointment and unfulfilled desire racked her body as he continued to knock. "We can sort this out, sweetheart. Please don't hide from me." The knocking paused, followed by a deeper thud as he put his shoulder to the thick planks. "Rory! It's not your fault, darling. It's mine!"

How can it be his fault? He's clearly had sex before. Lots of sex with women who knew what they were doing. With women whose bodies responded properly, who knew how to say the right thing. Jealousy oozed through her veins, black and bitter as coffee left too long in the pot. She threw her head back and screamed her frustration to the ceiling. The gods seemed to answer her as a crack of lightning lit up the cabin interior. A boom of thunder followed close behind, and rain rattled like bullets against the windows as a spring storm rolled in from nowhere.

"Fuck!" Sander banged his fist again. "Come on, Rory, please. I'm getting soaked out here."

"Your truck is right there. Get in it and just go home. We can pretend this never happened." She'd grown used to pretending over the years. She could get past this if he would just go away and leave her alone, give her time to think.

A furious roar split the air, drowning out the thunder as he body-slammed the wood so hard the hinges creaked. Rory squeaked and ducked beside the bed, flinching until she realized the old cabin had somehow survived his onslaught.

"Open this fucking door, Aurora! Right now!" A nearby window cracked as he rammed against the cabin again, followed by sudden silence. The storm continued to rage, bursts of lightning illuminating the cabin before plunging it back into darkness. Frozen in place, every sense straining against the fury of nature, she tried to ascertain whether he was still there. Ozone stung her nose, the pouring rain drowning any scents as she waited. A soft thud against the wood. "Let me in, honey, please. I swear I won't cross the threshold unless you say it's okay. I just need to see your face, Rory." He didn't sound angry, and his quiet plea drew her across the room.

She eased the bolt, twisted the lock, and opened the door a fraction, one hand clutching the blanket in place at her neck. The tang of iron hit her nose, a trace of blood, and she studied his soaking-wet form, trying to locate the source of injury. His brown hair lay plastered to his scalp, water dripping from it to run down his upper torso.

Her eyes chased a rivulet as it rolled over the sculpted abs on his lower body to disappear in the dark hair shadowing his cock. His flesh twitched under her scrutiny, and she turned her eyes away to study instead the knuckles of his hand, resting at his hip. The skin was torn and ragged, the source of the blood she smelled.

He raised his hand, studying the scratches with a look that said he hadn't noticed the injury until just then. He lifted it higher, pressing the palm against his nose, and drew a shuddering breath. "The scent of you belongs on my skin, Rory." His dark voice, full of sin and promise, rumbled in his chest.

"Why didn't you just leave?

"Because you never told me to." Gold flashed in his eyes. *Tricky wolf. What game is he playing?* She cocked her head and studied him, not liking the hint of a smile teasing around his mouth.

"I told you to go home." She scowled to hide her confusion.

"Then you'd better let me in, honey, because I am home." There it was again. The absolute certainty of tone made her head spin at the implication of his words.

Her hand fell away from the door, and it swung open as she retreated. Sander stayed in place. Every line and muscle in his body straining, he waited. "We went from zero to infinity in less than five minutes, darling. I lost control of the 'love rocket' for a moment there." The gentle words soothed her somewhat, but embarrassment at the reminder of her failing still stained her cheeks.

"You can come in, as long as you promise to forget I ever said that." She winced. Closing the distance between them, he pushed the door shut behind him. He chuckled, brushing the hair away from her forehead to press a kiss there.

"Aurora Jane Hanson, I am never going to forget your first foray into dirty talking." His sweet smile negated the potential sting of his words. He was teasing her; the way lovers did.

"I don't know what to do, you don't....we don't fit." The admission didn't cost as much as she feared when he cupped her chin in his hands. Soft lips brushed against hers, a feather-light touch he repeated again and again. Different from the hard, lusty touches they had shared earlier, she opened like a flower when his tongue brushed the seam of her mouth. His hold on her face stayed gentle, as though she were a piece of exquisite glass that would shatter under too much pressure. Teasing, questing, his tongue was never still as he explored every inch of her mouth, inviting her to join the dance.

Clutching at his shoulder, she ignored the blanket as it slid free. Copying his movements, she stroked the roof of his mouth as their bodies edged closer until they stood hip to hip. She rubbed against him, eager to please, to atone for the earlier mistakes, but he held her still.

"Shh," he breathed against her lips. "Just this is enough."

Chapter Seven

T he rhythmic *thunk, thunk, thunk* of an industrial stapler competed with shouted conversations, hammering, and the buzz of a grinder as Sander stopped the group of teens at the perimeter of the construction site. Work had progressed at a remarkable rate as more and more of the pack donated their time to the project. After the dark days of winter, everyone was keen to play their part in bringing the new hall to fruition.

The building was framed and watertight with first-fix utilities well under way. A cherry picker was secured behind barriers on the west side of the building as a team worked to fit solar panels to the roof. Sander pointed out the key risks to the six teens as they waited for permission from Stefan to enter the building.

A schedule had been agreed with Adrie. Sander would work with them two afternoons a week, and the site visit was their first field trip. Each of the kids had been assigned a support role for the dance preparations depending on aptitude and interest. Keeley, a petite blonde, was busy making notes on a pad as she strolled the perimeter of the visitor area. Her looks and size belied the fierce nature of her wolf, and she'd been thrilled when he asked for her input on the security preparations.

One of the boys, Adam, had shown an interest in the catering, and Sander had played the family card, getting him a part-time job at the restaurant. It was mostly bussing tables and washing up, but the boy seemed happy to earn a few bucks and had positively glowed when he'd told Sander about Will consulting him on the menu for the party. The other three, two boys and a girl, had been happy with assignment to the decorating team, and Rory was expected any time to join the tour of the hall.

He had a special project in mind for Daniel. Although he still hadn't contributed much to the discussions, he'd stayed behind the previous week to request the family photographs for the portrait. They'd agreed on a price of two hundred dollars. Well, Sander had offered, and the boy had stammered before gratefully accepting.

Sweet fruit and vanilla drifted on the breeze, and he spun like a compass toward his true north as Rory approached the small gathering. Her blonde curls were their usual tangle, and her well-worn jeans had a patch at the knee. A stripe of dirt decorated one cheek. She looked perfect to him. His wolf grumbled when she hung back at the edge of the group, and Sander concurred. Uncaring of the stares from the teens, he swooped down on her, smothering her protests in a kiss that left them both panting when they finally broke apart. Color bloomed on her cheeks as she scowled at him, but she pressed into his side when he curled his arm around her waist.

"Now I understand why your bed hasn't been slept in lately." His brother's dry voice elicited another round of giggles from the group. Sander shrugged, cheeks stretched wide by his grin as they made their way inside the building. Hard hats were issued to everyone, although the crew had stood down for a break for the duration of the tour.

Stefan took charge, showing them the main hall, the rooms designated for kitchen and bathroom facilities. The skeleton of a flight of stairs showed the route to the first floor, which would accommodate a group of meeting rooms as well as lead to a balcony circling the hall. The partial mezzanine had been added after Sander's request for the youth club space. The tour culminated in the large space at the rear of the complex reserved for the teens and younger adults. A separate entrance had been installed, and the kids oohed and aahed as they explored every inch.

The group thinned out as Rory led her team to the hall to take measurements. Keeley asked Stefan to show her around the site again, focusing on access points as part of her security assignment. Sander gave Adam permission to take some pictures in the unfinished kitchen area before he headed to the restaurant for his afternoon shift. Which just left Daniel. The boy checked his watch nervously. The worried scent that clung to the boy too often for Sander's liking threaded the air.

"There's plenty of time, Daniel. I promise I won't make you late home, but I have another commission for you." Cautious interest filled the boy's eyes as he moved closer at Sander's urging. "I want you to design and paint a mural." He gestured to the long white wall stretching the length of the room. "The design will be up to you, but I want it to reflect the pack. You guys are the future, and I want something to remind every person who looks at this wall what we are striving for."

He watched the idea take root, saw in the narrowing of Daniel's eyes how it spoke to him. The boy stepped closer, his hand trailing over the clean, blank surface, pausing here and there to trace an outline with one finger. "It's way bigger than anything I've done before," he breathed. Which was as good as saying yes, in Sander's book. Resisting the urge to clench his fist, he slung his arm around the boy's shoulders, steering him toward the reception area where Stefan waited with a roll of graph paper under his arm.

Sander left his brother to explain the dimensions to Daniel, how the grid on the paper could be projected onto the wall, giving him a reference to scale up his design. He wandered instead toward the main hall, meeting Rory on the way out as she herded her chattering group before her. He gave her a wink, indicating with his head he would wait for her to finish up. She flashed him a quick smile as she tried to focus on the excited suggestions from her enthusiastic helpers. The interaction was good for her, he could tell by the light in her aqua eyes as they flitted from child to child. With a laugh and a shooing motion, she eventually sent them on their way, agreeing to meet them the following week to review their suggestions. Propping her fists on her hips, she blew out a breath, giving him a tired smile. "I'm exhausted, I don't know how you keep up with them." Shaking her head, she hooked her arm through his as they strolled toward the exit, passing Stefan on the way out. He dropped his hand, having just waved Daniel off, and it delighted Sander to see the bounce in the boy's step as he hurried away.

"Good kid," Stefan observed, his grin turning sly as he studied his brother and his old friend arm in arm. "Hey, Rory, you better pay Margie a visit real soon. I reckon you gals will have a lot to talk about." Laughter echoing around the reception area, he brushed past them and returned to work.

Lowering his head, Sander buried it in her hair, loving the sweet scent perfuming the curls. He'd been spending every night at Rory's, taking things slow and easy. Sharing kisses and light caresses only. He was determined to give her time to learn what she wanted, find out what she liked rather than following his more experienced lead. His dick was refusing to talk to him, and he'd become adept at sleeping with a hard-on, but it didn't matter. She was his mate, and if he had to wait a while before he fully claimed her, then so be it. Didn't mean he couldn't ramp up their play a little.

The youngsters had taken him on a tour of pack lands, showing him the places they liked to hang out, including the water hole they favored during the hot summer months. Surrounded by rocks, with a rope swing hanging from the branches of an old tree, it was a great place to let off steam. They'd also taken him through the woods to a familiar spot, proving some things never changed. The old shack he remembered was long gone, but a new one stood in its place. According to the kids, the alpha had built it as a present for his mate, Betty. Sander had some good memories of the old shack, and the visit with the kids had inspired him. Tugging Rory by the hand, he ignored her laughing protests and loped off into the woods. The structure was simple, though crafted with skill, Drew having worked as a carpenter to support himself while banished from the pack. The alpha had also found time to put in a few hours working on the hall, prompting several other pack members to volunteer their time.

Sander knocked on the door of the shack and listened for a moment before turning the handle and ushering Rory inside. She took a few steps into the small building before turning to face him with a confused expression. He closed the door, slid the bolt, and pressed his back to it as he studied her. "What...what are we doing here?" she said, glancing around the room. An old rug covered the floor. Plush cushions and a couple of old beanbag chairs were piled in one corner. A shelf on the wall held a multitude of candles, some barely started, others merely stumps of melted wax. Nothing matched, and it was clear things had been added here and there by different people. Eyes narrowed, she rounded on him. "Did you bring me to a make-out spot?"

Grabbing a few large pillows, he laid them in the center of the rug and flopped down upon them, patting the space next to him. "Come on, Rory, come and play with me. I've been thinking about you all day." He growled low in his throat. Spots of color decorated her cheekbones as she nibbled at her lower lip. She looked shy and completely sexy in her old flannel shirt and faded denim. The women he'd dated casually over the years had all been a type—sleek, sophisticated, cold as ice. Nothing like this scruffy she-wolf who was rapidly becoming his only obsession.

He sat up, eyes fixed on his mate as his wolf came to the fore. Letting their desire for her shine hot in his gaze, he slowly unbuttoned his blue cotton shirt, sliding it from his shoulders. "Now your turn, honey," he coaxed.

Although she rolled her eyes and laughed, it didn't stop her slipping loose the first couple of buttons on the flannel, giving him a hint of what looked suspiciously like black lace. The thought of his practical, no-nonsense woman decked out in something other than plain white cotton swelled his cock to unbearable hardness. On hands and knees, he stalked her across the rug.

"Uh, uh, uh." Her wagging finger stopped him in his tracks. She turned her back on him. Red-and-black checks glided down to reveal an expanse of creamy skin stretched over the subtly sculpted muscles of her upper back. The black straps of her bra stood out starkly as she dropped her hands behind her, letting the shirt fall free. He watched, mesmerized as Rory lifted her arms to gather the mass of her curly hair. Her clasped hands slid higher to cup the back of her head, displaying the delicate column of her neck. The dip of her waist, the definition of her biceps, the utter sensuality of her pose destroyed his control.

"Turn around, honey." His guttural growl more wolf than man, he held his breath as she obeyed. The arch in her spine lifted her breasts, causing her stiff nipples to poke through the lacy cups of her bra. She angled her head away, baring her throat, inviting him to suck hard on the pulse throbbing there. "Come here," he whispered, reaching up to catch her around the waist as she lowered to her knees.

He held her in place, bending his head to capture her left breast with his mouth. A soft moan teased his ears. He sucked harder, drawing as much of her flesh between his lips as he could. Loving the little sounds of pleasure she made, he plied his tongue over her nipple, using the lace covering her skin to increase sensation. Rory dropped her hands to his head, pressing him closer, and he relished the prick of her short nails on his scalp.

Watching her confidence bloom over their shared nights of play had been an exquisite pleasure, proving he'd been right to take things back to basics. He'd forgotten over the years how much fun the slow burn of foreplay could be.

Keeping his mouth fixed on her breast, he unbuttoned her jeans, praying to the gods a matching pair of panties hid beneath them. The feel of warm, naked skin under his hands fired such a bolt of lust to his groin, his eyes crossed as he battled not to come. Releasing her breast, he rested his head on her flat stomach, staring down at the sheer black thong covering her pussy. "Are you trying to kill me?" he muttered hoarsely, and the laugh she gave spoke of a woman enjoying her sexuality. With a mock snarl, he sank his teeth into the ripe curve of her hip, cupping her pubic bone so his fingers rested over the damp silk between her thighs.

"Sander." His name on her lips was a sigh, a plea, a benediction as he lowered her onto her back. He tugged the thong and her jeans free until she was naked except for her bra. Exerting gentle pressure to her knees, he spread her thighs, laying her open before his greedy eyes. A dusting of blonde curls framed her sex, arousal glistening between the folds. The sweet fragrance of her passion hit like a drug to his senses. Unable to fight the need to taste her, he thrust his hands under her ass, lifting her hips to meet his mouth.

Sharp, sweet, with just a hint of salt, her essence coated his tongue as he buried it deep in her pussy. Her hands gripped his hair, trying to tug him away as she gasped in shock at the sudden invasion. Refusing to yield, he shifted his mouth to suck her clit, teasing the tight bundle until the pressure from her fingers relaxed and dropped away. He growled his approval, knowing the vibrations would further stimulate her, and she cried out, bucking against his face.

Wetness coated his chin, and he slid lower to gather her cream with long, deep licks. Raising his eyes, he stared up her body, continuing to lap at her. Her breasts heaved as she panted, and the muscles of her stomach pulled taut as she lifted her hips in offering. Turning his head, he bit the inside of her thigh before sitting back on his heels. She whimpered at the loss of his tongue, and he replaced it with a thick finger, pressing slow and deep before withdrawing to circle the entrance of her pussy. "Feeling good, darling?" he murmured, and she hummed softly, rocking her hips so the heel of his hand rubbed against her clit.

Adding another finger, he worked her open. Thrusting and twisting, he leaned forward, increasing the pressure of his palm. He braced himself with his other hand, resting it beside her head. Aqua eyes met his as he fixed his mouth on hers. Sharing her taste, he mimicked the action of his fingers with his tongue. Nails scratching at his shoulders, she clutched him closer, moaning her pleasure into his mouth.

Her hips faltered, losing their rhythm, and he knew she was close. Pulling free, he shifted his attention to the curve of her neck. "Come for me," he demanded, biting down on the tender flesh at the top of her shoulder. The dominant command all she needed, she turned into his cheek, muffling a scream as she fell over the edge.

A heavy fist thumped against the wooden door. Sander jerked away, crouching over his vulnerable mate, snarling in fury at the intrusion. "Hey! You kids need to cool off." The deep rumbling voice was unmistakable. With a squeak of horror, Rory wriggled out from under Sander and scrambled into her shirt.

The knock came again, and she whispered, "Pants, where are my pants?"

A laugh burst from his mouth.

"It's not funny!" she hissed, glaring at him as she thrust her legs into her jeans.

"It kind of is," he replied, moving to the door, checking she was decently covered before undoing the bolt. Leaning against the doorframe, he crossed his arms over his bare chest, making sure to block the entrance as much as possible. "Hey, Gee. What's up?"

The big bear blinked a couple of times, impressing Sander with his composure. "Hey, Sander. Just wanted to say it's good to have you back in town." A muscle in Gee's cheek twitched when an embarrassed whimper came from within the shack. "Well, hopefully I'll see you guys at The Den sometime soon. First round's on me." With a nod, and a quick "See ya, Rory," Gee moved off shaking his head and muttering, "What is it with that Burrows family? Why can't they find a nice comfortable bed, like normal wolves?"

Sander spun on his heel, laughing as he watched Rory shake her leg until her thong slid out of the bottom of her jeans. "So you ready to try for a home run?" He grinned, ducking a cushion whizzing toward his head. "Rain check?"

Her scream echoed around the shack. *Maybe not....*

Chapter Eight

The dance was two weeks away and Rory was at the end of her tether with "helpful" suggestions regarding the decoration of the hall. She was beginning to wish she had stood firm against the matrons and refused to be involved. *Yeah, like that was even an option.* Between the bickering at the committee meetings and the rising sexual tension between herself and Sander, her head spun.

He'd been patient with her, infuriatingly so at times, but he didn't seem in any hurry to claim her. The insecure young girl haunted the back of her mind, worried he didn't feel the same connection. The urge to claim him, to pour forth the words of love in her heart intensified every day, but fear of rejection held her mute. With a sigh, she bent her head to the task of twisting thick wire to form the framework of the huge wreath that would hang suspended from the upper-floor balcony of the hall. Her student volunteers were working on longer looping frames that would garland either side of the wreath.

It was Saturday morning, and she had been surprised when the teens turned up early to help. Other members of the pack passed through, wanting a peek at the almost-completed structure. It was a pleasing sign of the positive improvements within the pack how many sat down to lend a hand. Before she knew it, she had a regular production line going.

The theme of the dance was renewal. A traditional spring theme as Rory wanted to acknowledge the history of the dance, tracing it back to its earliest time as a rite to appeal to the spirits for their blessing on the new season's plantings. The recent resurrection of the Winter Solstice celebrations had been a success in spite of the horrors that had followed soon after. The alpha was keen to continue with events to bind the pack closer together. It had only been a year since his return, and old hurts and bad memories would take a long time to heal.

A pack run had been called for that evening, another example of the unifying activities being reintroduced. The human half of their natures had seen Drew heal from his gunshot wound, but the wolves needed to see their alpha, too. Run with him, hunt with him, mark their territory anew with the melded scents of family and home. It had been a long time since Rory had been on a pack run, and she was nervous in the extreme. The injury to her right hand was less obvious in human form, but she couldn't disguise it when she ran as a wolf. Limped as a wolf, more accurately, as the missing claws made it hard for her to distribute her weight.

She'd been invited to join the Burrows, shift at their home, and meet up with the rest of the pack as part of their group. Hannah would stay at home with Bridie and Will who were closing the restaurant for the night. It was going to be Jessie's first run, and the little girl was beside herself with excitement, according to Sander. Most children didn't experience their first shift until they were older, but the healing that had saved the little girl's life had awoken the latent wolf genes in her heritage.

Her thoughts wandered as her fingers twisted and shaped the pliable wire. The kids chattered among themselves, the group expanding and contracting as people came and went. A shadow crossed over her, and she lifted her head as Stefan squatted beside her.

"Have you seen Daniel anywhere this morning?" he asked, a frown marring his brow. She pondered a moment before responding. A lot of people had passed through, and she sifted the images and scents in her recent memory.

"No, I can't recall him being around this morning. Have you asked the others?" She nodded toward her teens. When he confirmed he had, she offered another alternative. "Maybe he's with Sander." As though summoned by her mention of his name, the fresh wintergreen scent that stirred her body and soul swirled in the air. Wolf and woman locked immediately on the source as Sander strode across the large room, his focus just as keen.

Uncaring of their audience, he went to one knee before her, cupping her face to press a kiss to her lips. The response within her drew a chuckle of very male satisfaction from him. He turned to his brother, clasping his shoulder in greeting. "Everything okay, Stefan?"

"I was just explaining to Rory, Daniel hasn't shown up this morning. I'd arranged to help him with the transfer of his mural onto the wall." He paused, sighing briefly. "This is the third meeting he's missed."

Concern laced her mate's scent as he rose abruptly, shoving his hands on his hips as he huffed out a breath. "I'm guessing there's an issue with his mom. I don't know the full story, but she seems to be on her own with Daniel and a couple of little ones. I'd better go over there and check on him."

Rory scrambled to her feet. Placing her hand on his chest, she looked into his eyes. "You're really worried, aren't you?"

He nodded.

"I'll come with you. We've achieved a lot more than I expected, thanks to so many volunteers." Hand in hand, they moved through the hall, Rory pausing to thank various people on the way.

Their route took them along Main Street, busy with pack members shopping, browsing, or just passing the time of day. Another sign of the returning health of their community. Two groups met in a laughing tangle at the entrance to the convenience store, performing that universal left-right sidestep as they tried to pass each other. A small boy toddled free of the group, wobbling toward the steps. With a shout of alarm, Rory dashed forward, scooping up the little boy moments before he tumbled off the top step. The little darling giggled and patted her cheek, seemingly oblivious to the danger he'd been in.

"Oh, Cody!" a woman cried as she hurried toward her, snatching the child from Rory's arms. Cody's mother turned without a word of thanks to yell at the familiar teenager struggling to control an identical small boy, clearly Cody's twin. "Danny! What were you thinking? All I ask is for a little help, but you can't manage even the simplest of tasks!" The teen ducked his head, cheeks flushed, mumbling an apology as he finally got his little charge under control.

Rory glanced up at Sander. His arms were folded and a soft growl rumbled in his throat. Casual observers took note of his hostile body language and moved away, leaving them isolated on the steps of the store. The woman's tirade trailed off and she spun to face them. Dark-purple smudges lay heavy beneath her brown eyes, lines of tension furrowing her brow and bracketing the sides of her mouth. Her light-brown hair fell in a limp tail down her back, her scent heavy with stress. Julia Maddox looked older than her forty-eight years, a rare occurrence in wolves owing to their extended life-span. A scowl further darkened her features as she thrust the toddler at her elder son and started to herd her family down the steps.

"We missed you at the youth club today, Daniel." The ice in Sander's tone was unlike anything Rory had heard before, and she placed a restraining hand on his arm.

"He doesn't have time for nonsense like that," Julia snapped, giving her son a small push when he would have stopped to talk. *Poor kid.* Rory's heart ached as Daniel curled in upon himself, steering his little brothers away.

"He has real talent, Ms. Maddox—"

Julia snarled and rounded on him. "Talent doesn't put food on the table. Talent doesn't help me pay our bills. I need Daniel at home, minding the twins, not messing around with pencils and paint! As soon as school is over, he'll be out to work. Stop filling his head with stupid dreams of things that can't happen! Correspondence courses for art school?" she scoffed. "It's all well and good for the likes of you with plenty of money. He needs a job!" An ugly flush mottled her skin and tears glinted in her eyes as she railed at him.

Rory stepped forward, wanting to comfort her distressed pack mate, but Julia shook her off. "You weren't here, Sander Burrows! You don't know what it's been like! You think you can just waltz back into town and tell me how to raise my child?" Her voice was shrill, tears coursing down her cheeks. "Why did *you* come back? Why did you come back and he didn't?" The words were barely intelligible through her sobs, and Rory caught her as she crumpled to the ground.

Familiar scents surrounded them as the matrons descended. Miss Claire stroked Julia's hair, whispering soothing words, Miss Fern crouching beside her. "Oh, Julia dear. Hush now, it'll be all right."

The elder wolves took the distressed woman in hand, and Rory eased her way out of the huddle, moving swiftly toward Daniel who stared in horror at his mother, the twins clinging to his legs. She touched each of the little ones on the head before stroking the boy's cheek.

"I know it hurts, Daniel, but this is for the best. Your mom has obviously been trying to do too much on her own, and that's not how pack is supposed to work." She glanced over her shoulder as Betty, the alpha's mate, joined the group. Daniel whined, and Rory patted his back. "Now the betas are aware of things, they'll make sure your mom has all the support she needs."

"It's my fault, though. I let her down by being selfish...." The words were barely audible, but they hurt her heart.

"Daniel, sweetheart, it's not your fault. None of this is your fault. Magnum did this, not you. He tore so many families apart, just like yours." The boy's breath hitched and he pressed his forehead into Rory's shoulder. She rubbed his back, watching Sander who stood deep in conversation with Miss Kathy. As though feeling her stare, he glanced up, his eyes raw with pain. Her wolf surged, desperate to comfort their mate, but the boy she held needed her support more than the man. She nodded to show him Daniel was okay, and Sander turned his attention back to the fierce old woman.

Knowing her friends would support her, she drew back until Daniel raised his wet face. Brushing the tears away with the back of her hand, she smiled. "The pack run is tonight." Daniel nodded hesitantly, looking down at his little brothers who were patting and rubbing his legs as they tried to comfort him. "You and your mom will run with us tonight. Bring the boys to the Burrows' house, Hannah will watch over them. She'll have Will and Bridie to help her. Your mom knows them, doesn't she?"

Hope bloomed in his expression, and Rory battled to hold in a sigh. This little family had come too close to slipping through the cracks. She'd been selfish herself, keeping the pack at arm's length, interacting when she chose to. Like so many others, self-preservation had taken priority over the needs of the pack. It was time to stop letting fear rule their lives. They would only thrive and heal when everyone played their part, including her.

***

The small blonde wolf shook vigorously, settling her fur as she adjusted from the shift. A thick muzzle rubbed along hers as the huge gray wolf turned from his protective stance to press against her. Sander towered over her in both forms, and she leaned her weight against his solid body as he *whuffed* and curled his head over her back, pressing her closer.

An even-larger gray wolf nudged a petite russet female behind him. Rory lolled her tongue out in a laugh when the little omega nipped her mate on the tail. Ven had similar coloring to the other males, Caitlyn a smaller version of her mother's red wolf form. A little brown pup gamboled from adult to adult, each one lowering to touch noses, scent marking their precious child. A shy pair of light-brown wolves were encouraged forward by Marjorie, as Julia and Daniel joined them. Stefan took point, his mate at his side, and the rest of the wolves formed a group around Caleb and Jessie. Ven took the rear, Caitlyn directly in front of him, and they moved off, loping toward the main meeting point for the run.

The moon hung low and full in the sky, watching over her children as wolves poured from every direction to gather around the pair of black wolves at the very center of the group—the alpha and his mate. The pack ebbed and swelled like a living being as they turned and mingled, greeting friends, noting the location of others who might challenge for dominance.

Excitement painted the air as anticipation built, muscles bunched as the wolves watched and waited for the signal. Satisfied the pack was gathered, Drew threw back his head and loosed a howl which was picked up and echoed by all present. The eerie song rippled through the woods, a warning to their prey to flee, a challenge to other predators. The Tao Pack would brook no threats. As one, the wolves surged forward, flowing like water over the land.

This was home. Written in every rock and tree, the song of the pack hummed beneath their paws as they roamed wide and free across their territory, renewing their bonds with the nurturing soil. Scents and sounds combined as the pack raced through their home. Splitting into smaller groups, they spread out in all directions. Rory's heart beat fast as the ground fell away beneath her paws, breath misting in the cool night air. The essence of family surrounded her, Sander never far from her side as the group stayed together. Daniel surged forward, bracketed by Stefan and Caleb while the females closed around Jessie. The boy's excited yip echoed through the trees when a rabbit dashed from cover and he leapt in pursuit.

The trickle of a stream over rocks called to them, and they paused to rest, lapping at the icy-cold water. The trio of males would return once Daniel had captured or lost his prey. Sander and Ven positioned themselves to guard the females and the cub, relaxed but attentive. Rory took her turn at the stream and Marjorie curled on the ground, Jessie slumped tired but happy against her flank.

An unwelcome scent caught Rory's attention,

sharp like green apples. She turned, snarling at a pale-gray wolf who stepped daintily from beneath the trees too close to Sander. Rory's hackles rose as wolf and woman gave name to the threat—*Carolina*. A contemporary from their youth. Beautiful, confident, and an utter bitch in both forms. Rory's lips drew back, baring her sharp teeth at the trespasser. Fury surged in her blood as Rory darted forward to snap at Carolina when she stepped too close to her mate. Forcing the female back, she assumed a blocking stance, her body shielding Sander. She snarled again. The gray circled, feinting forward to nip at Rory's flank, but she held her position, raising a paw to swipe her opponent's muzzle when she moved too slowly.

The gray yipped, turned and charged, aiming deliberately for Rory's weaker front right leg. The blow staggered her, but she was used to carrying most of her weight on three paws and didn't go down. This wasn't the first time the other female had challenged her. Carolina had a reputation as a bully using her superior strength against wolves she deemed inferior. She'd been the same when they were growing up, teasing and taunting with words as well as her claws. She also wasn't particularly bright, and her attacks lacked variety, so Rory knew what to expect.

A deep growl vibrated behind her, and she flicked her head to snarl at Sander. *Our fight.* Carolina tried to take advantage of what she assumed was Rory's momentary distraction and darted forward again. Ducking down, Rory avoided the body blow from the bigger wolf, taking Carolina's legs out from beneath her instead. Spinning, she used her back legs to spring forward, slamming into her attacker. Her surprise retaliation succeeded in knocking the wind out of Carolina who struggled to stand. Like most bullies, Carolina hadn't expected much of a challenge, but Rory had something worth fighting for now. A reassuring weight rested against her side after Sander moved closer to stand beside her. They confronted the intruder as a united front, a pair, a partnership. The female whined before disappearing into the tree line.

Chapter Nine

Adrenaline and lust surging in his veins, Sander battled to focus on the bumpy lane to their cabin. The sight of his shy little Rory staking her claim to him did fierce things to his heart. Primal need threatened to strip away the layers of civility leaving only the beast living in the core of his being. He'd had it in his mind to wait for the night of the dance to claim Rory, but his wolf had other ideas. He stopped the truck at the edge of the clearing and turned off the engine. Gripping the wheel between his fingers, he didn't dare look at her as he spoke between gritted teeth. "I want you, Rory. I want you, and the wolf wants you. I'm right at the edge of my control, so you need to decide. Tell me no and I'll leave, but I need to do it now." The leather creaked beneath his hands, and he released the wheel before he did any permanent damage to the vehicle.

Cranberries and vanilla bloomed in the small space, undercut with the musky scent of arousal. He clenched his fists, focusing on her scent, sifting the layers as he sought any trace of fear or uncertainty. He needed this to go right, had planned a careful seduction of his mate down to the last detail. Rutting on her like a dog in heat was definitely not part of the plan. A soft caress over his balled fists drew his gaze and a shudder rippled his spine as she traced a gentle pattern with two fingers and her thumb. The fact she had reached for him with her damaged hand flayed him open. His Rory trusted him with everything, including her weaknesses.

He climbed from the truck, circling the hood to ease open her door. She turned in her seat, a soft smile on her lips. A banked heat matching his glowed in her eyes. She raised her arms, and he bent forward to lift her, her legs snaking around his hips until she clung to the front of his body. Cupping the soft, warm cheeks of her ass, he carried her toward the cabin, trying to ignore the heat from her core searing his cock through their thin clothing.

Sharp teeth nipped his throat and he dropped to his knees in the damp grass of the clearing. "Rory. *Rory.*" His voice was guttural as she squirmed in his lap, her mouth busy on his skin. "Not here, not like this, honey," he groaned, fingers flexing convulsively on her ripe curves.

"Yes, Sander. Yes. Here. Just like this. I want to feel the land beneath me, the light of the moon on us." She moaned, rocking her hips against him, and his control snapped. His claws shredded the thin top and yoga pants in seconds, baring her breasts to his seeking mouth as he bore her to the ground. The scents of crushed grass and herbs surrounded them as he pulled back to strip his clothing. Rory raised herself on her elbows to watch him, her wolf's closeness making the aqua of her eyes glow with an incandescent light. Her thighs were splayed open, her breasts thrusting forward, she offered herself to him, freely and without hesitation. Saliva pooling in his mouth at the sight of her, he stretched his body over hers. Soft skin met hard muscle, their mouths fused, and his cock came to rest against the wet heat of her core.

The need to claim rode him, and he pressed his tongue between her lips, thrusting hard the way he longed to thrust into her pussy. She moaned into his mouth. Blunt nails digging into his shoulders, she pulled him closer, taking what he gave her without resistance. Sweat slicked their skin as they rubbed together, and he rolled onto his back to avoid crushing her with his weight. Rory straddled him, messy hair tumbling around her shoulders. She braced her small hands against her chest, catching her breath. She looked glorious in the moonlight; her plump breasts dangled invitingly. Reaching to cup them, he teased her nipples with the calloused skin of his thumbs. She arched her back, grinding her wet core against him, and he bit the inside of his cheek, trying to retain a shred of control. He forced his legs to remain lax, fighting the urge to raise his knees and tip her pelvis forward to where he needed her to be.

With a wicked smile, she eased from his touch, scooting down his body. He scrambled to reach her, to pull her away, but she was too quick, sucking the head of his cock into the hot depths of her mouth. Fingers that had meant to restrain suddenly pressed her closer as the slick, wet caress of her tongue flickered over and around the tip. Sweat broke out on his brow as she hollowed her cheeks, sucking hard with more enthusiasm than finesse.

The naivety of her touch was enough to rein him

back. Forcing his hands to relax by his sides, he let his mate explore at her pace for a few moments. Her clever little tongue traced the length of him, curling and teasing just beneath the head until he bucked his hips. "Enough, Rory," he growled, and she pulled back, uncertainty painted in her eyes.

"Did I do something wrong?" He hated she even had to ask, and he shook his head quickly. "It's too good, honey. The feel of your mouth on me is just too damn good," he reassured her as he flipped her onto her back and knelt between her legs. Using his left hand, he spread her open, sliding the first two digits of his right hand easily inside her pussy. She was used to his touch now, and she rolled her hips, seeking the pressure of his thumb against her clit.

He pumped his hand, scissoring his fingers apart to gently stretch her further before slipping a third in. Her muscles clenched momentarily and he paused, lowering his mouth to tease one nipple until she moaned and rocked her body. He held still, letting her fuck herself on his hand as he bit down hard on the side of her breast. She cried out, core rippling as she came, cream flowing from her pussy to coat his palm.

Stroking and petting, Sander eased Rory through the vestiges of her orgasm until she collapsed against the cool grass and sighed. Her cheeks were flushed, eyes bright as they fixed on his, and she smiled lazily. "We're getting pretty good at this," she noted, and he chuckled in spite of the fire raging in his body.

He leaned forward, bracing one hand beside her head as he gripped the base of his cock with the other. "Lift your hips for me, honey," he whispered, and, eyes wide, she moved to comply. His cock slicked through her pussy a couple of times before he found the right angle and eased inside. She grunted, but didn't protest, as he pressed forward until the entire head of his cock bathed in her molten heat.

Grinding his teeth, he waited, calling on every ounce of his determination to not thrust until she was ready. Her hands relaxed on his hips finally, shifting to stroke tentatively over the taut cheeks of his ass, and he groaned in relief. With infinite patience, he pressed forward until she rolled her hips and the full length of him slid home.

Pressing his mouth to hers, Sander kissed her deeply, using his tongue to distract her while she adjusted to his invasion. He nipped her lower lip, across her cheek, along her jaw, until he found the soft skin at the curve of her neck. Sliding his hips back, he groaned as her muscles gripped him and he rocked gently forward again. The slow pace was killing him, but he would at least die a happy man, buried to the hilt in his mate.

"Can I move, too?" The sweet words brought a feral grin to his mouth. He shifted his hands to curl them under her ass.

"You can do anything you want, my darling. Anything—" He groaned when she hooked her legs around his hips and thrust up to meet his downward stroke. Like a hound slipping the leash, he loosed his control and powered into her, letting all his passion for her fill his heart as he rode her into the grass.

His wolf howled in his mind as their mate cried out, her core fluttering around him as she came again. The heat boiled through him. He thrust one last time, teeth seeking the soft flesh of her shoulder. The tang of her blood on his tongue blew his mind.

Pumping hard, he shot his seed deep into her core. She cried out, convulsing around him as he staked his claim, took his mate, and marked her forever as his.

His bones turned to rubber, and he had just enough awareness to fall sideways, twisting Rory in his arms so she lay panting against his chest. The cold dampness of the ground eventually registered against his back, and he opened his eyes to find his mate staring at him, her chin propped on her hands. "I need a shower, Sander," she said with a grin which ended on a laugh as he flowed to his feet, scooping her up in arms.

Glancing down, he noticed where they'd been lying. "We made a mess of your garden, honey." Looking up he saw flecks of green and brown in her hair and on her cheek. "Looks like I made a mess of you, too."

She curled her arms around his neck, pressing her nipples against his chest as he carried her toward the cabin. "Get me in a hot shower and then we can make a mess of our bed," she promised.

***

The clock on the dashboard clicked inexorably around to the half hour, and Sander checked it against the watch at his wrist. Sitting in the dark shadows across from the bus station in Rapid City was not where he wanted to be right now. He wanted to be holding Rory close in his arms as they swayed to the music. It was the night of the spring dance, and he was miles from home.

They had hardly seen each other, apart from at night as the final preparations for the dance took most of their time. When he hadn't been busy with the security arrangements, he'd been working with the teens and beginning a slow outreach to the younger adults in the pack. He'd also taken on a personal project which ate into what little free time remained. Chasing down leads with the help of a few trusted members of the pack, he hadn't expected a result so quickly. His hunt looked like it was going to pay off, which was why he lurked in his current spot.

A bus swung into the station, and he craned forward to read the number above the driver. Not the one he was waiting for. He sat back with a sigh, resisting the urge to check his watch again. *She's going to kill me for this.*

Chapter Ten

Rory closed her eyes against the wave of anger and disappointment as Stefan helped her from the truck. She forced a smile as Marjorie bent to brush a crease from the skirt of Rory's aqua-and-cream dress. The garment was the most delicate thing she had ever worn, and it was driving her crazy. The fitted bodice was laced tight, forcing her breasts up until she feared they would spill from the neckline. The skirt fell in a mass of tiny pleats from the waistline to mid-calf, the extra material causing it to spin every time she turned too quickly. Her feet had been squeezed, under great protest, into a pair of kitten heels which looked fabulous and hurt like the devil. She planned to kick the evil things under the table the moment she sat down. Marjorie slapped her hand away as she raised it to touch the unfamiliar waves of hair cascading past her shoulders.

It had taken both Margie and Hannah the best part of an hour to tease out every knot and tangle, followed by another hour letting the conditioning treatment they slathered on her scalp go to work.

They'd painted her nails, plucked her eyebrows, and made up her face until Rory barely recognized her reflection. The fact she had submitted with the barest grumble stood testament to how much she wanted to please Sander when he walked into the hall with her on his arm.

Instead, she found herself mirroring her best friend as Stefan placed them on either side of him, an exact replica of their entrance to the dance all those years ago. Her fingers tightened on Stefan's arm, and he bent his head to whisper, "He'll be here, Rory, I promise." It had taken every ounce of her friends' persuasion to get her in the truck once she found out Sander had been called away for an "emergency." The fact he had left without talking to her ignited all her childish insecurities.

A trio of people waited at the entrance to the hall, two females also flanking a male. Daniel looked sweetly handsome in a dark suit, his mother on one side and a startling young blonde in a red dress on the other. Rory hid her surprise when she recognized Keeley, the confident young dominant who Sander had recruited to help with security. She wouldn't have put the two together, but Keeley's hand curled around her classmate's biceps in a definite gesture of possession.

The boy looked past them, unable to hide his disappointment when he realized Sander wasn't with them. She wasn't the only person her mate had stood up. Stefan took charge of the group, explaining his brother had been unavoidably detained but would join them as soon as he could. He took them on a tour of the complex, for Julia and Marjorie's benefit mostly, but Rory was interested to hear him explain some of the innovative processes that had gone into the design and build.

Their walk culminated at the back of the building. Stefan rested his hand on the door to the youth club, turning his attention to the couple who moved to join them. "Drew, Betty." He inclined his head in a nod of respect at the alpha and his mate who smiled in return. Stefan gestured to Daniel, and Rory felt almost sorry for him as the ashen-faced boy stepped forward.

"I didn't expect this," he muttered, ducking his head.

"It's brilliant. *You're* brilliant." Keeley grasped his hand and squeezed tightly. "Show them, Danny."

At her urging, the teen opened the door to the youth club and Stefan ushered everyone inside the dark room. The lights flicked on, and there was a moment of breathless silence followed by gasps and laughter as they studied the exquisite mural stretching the length of the wall. Wolves covered the space. From golden eyes peeking from beneath the shadow of the trees, to a matched pair leading a hunting pack, their sable fur gleaming. There was even a little brown pup sipping from a small stream as a group of adults circled protectively around it.

A quiet sob silenced the group as they turned to watch Julia step up to the wall. She traced the flank of a gray wolf, teeth bared in a fierce snarl, as tears dripped unheeded down her cheeks. She wandered as though in a trance from scene to scene, fingers touching again and again until she finally turned to her son with a look of awe. "You did this?"

He nodded.

"I had no idea," she choked out, gathering him

against her.

The group moved away, giving the pair a semblance of privacy. Mother and son clung together, words of apology spilling from Julia as she cried on his shoulder. Rory swallowed the lump in her throat, wishing Sander could be there to witness the tender moment. *Where are you?*

The alpha and his mate heaped praise upon Daniel until the boy blushed so hard, he glowed like a tomato. Betty extracted a stammering promise he would recreate a smaller version of the black wolves for her before they left to join the main party.

It was Rory's turn to blush as they made their way into the hall as person after person stopped to tell her how much they loved the decorations. The wreath and garlands dominated the space, hanging above the stage. The metal frames had been stuffed with evergreen boughs, ivy, and spring flowers. Each table had a tall glass vase holding a spray of twigs hung with brightly decorated eggs, an ancient symbol of fertility and new life. Big tubs of spring bulbs— hyacinths, daffodils, and pansies, stood between the tables, adding splashes of color everywhere the eye fell.

The matrons held court at a large table on the left of the room, close to the area reserved for the dance floor. Rory tried to steer her friends to the other side of the hall, but Marjorie made a beeline for an empty table close to the elders. She waved and smiled at the foursome, returning their greetings. Miss Claire frowned at the empty seat next to Rory, turning to poke Miss Fern who looked ready to come over until Miss Kathy leaned toward them. After a hushed exchange, the women settled back, and a prickle of tension set between Rory's shoulder blades. Wherever her mate was, it appeared Miss Kathy was involved somehow.

***

Rory did her best to enjoy the dance. The lively music kept the floor filled with couples and groups of friends. Long trestle tables hugged the back wall, laden with food. She spotted Adam flitting from one end to the other as Will and Bridie kept him busy, and the teen looked in his element. *Another sight Sander should be enjoying.* Excusing herself from the table, she made her way to the restroom to freshen up. Her absence would also give Stefan and Marjorie the opportunity to dance together. Washing her hands, she kept her wrists under the cold water of the tap as she battled the tears pricking behind her eyes. It was nearly nine o'clock. He was over two hours late and bad memories were surfacing again.

What if he's left town? He did it before. There's nothing to stop him doing it again.

Rory patted her damp hands to her cheeks and gave herself a stern talking to. Things were different now. They were mated. She touched the fading mark at her throat, a talisman to help her hold her nerve. She'd woken that morning to his heated breath on the back of her neck as he slid gently into her, rocking them both to completion as the sun crept over the horizon. Drying her hands on a paper towel before digging the red lipstick Marjorie had loaned her out of her bag, she slicked it over her mouth. Squaring her shoulders, she left the bathroom, almost running into Carolina and a couple of her friends on their way in. The tall brunette sneered down her nose, stepping back as though contact with Rory would soil her outfit.

Rory stared hard at the other woman for a moment. Dealing with her was the last thing she needed. The hardness in her eyes prompted a flicker of wariness in Carolina's gaze before she covered it quickly.

"It must be déjà vu, for you." Carolina's voice dripped in sympathy, but she didn't fool Rory for a second. There was no way the woman would pass up an opportunity to get her own back, and she proved it with her next words. "At least, last time he stood you up, you had the good grace to go home. Poor Marjorie must be fed up with you hanging around like a bad smell."

Rory waited for the rush of embarrassment to heat her cheeks, but it never came. She really didn't care what this pathetic woman thought of her. Her friends and family were all that mattered. Sander was all that mattered. *He is a good mate; we can trust him.* The reassurance from her wolf stiffened her spine, and she stepped around the three women, intent on going back to the dance.

"Don't you walk away from me!" Sharp nails dug into her forearm as Carolina made a grab for her. Her voice was loud enough to draw attention, and people drifted from the main hall into the lobby. Rory watched them gather. Some of their expressions reflected concern but most were there to enjoy the spectacle.

"Take your hand off me, Carolina." The colors and shades of the lobby shifted as her wolf surged forward, her voice a growled threat. "I'll only tell you once." She refused to turn, giving her back to the other woman in a deliberate insult. She held still, although her wolf snarled at the restraining hold.

"Rory."

The watching eyes, the sharp nails stinging her arm, old ghosts trying to shred her confidence were all forgotten as her mate called to her. Shaking off Carolina, she turned toward the open door as a familiar silhouette came into focus and Sander stepped into the lobby. He looked gorgeous. His charcoal pinstriped suit darkened his eyes to slate. A tall blond man, notable for his casual clothes amongst all the finery, stood just behind him.

Sander ushered the man forward and a gasp rose from the small crowd behind Rory, followed by a sob of disbelief. "*Erik?*"

The man dropped his rucksack on the floor and flew across the lobby, catching the crying woman tight against him. "Julia. Julia." He pressed his lips against her hair as they rocked together, tears flowing.

"Dad!" Daniel hurled himself at the pair, and they opened their arms to cuddle their son close.

Rory started at the brush against her cheek, turning into the warm strength of her mate. "I'm sorry, honey." He kissed her brow, her cheek, her jaw, as she pressed against the hard heat of his body.

"You're here now," she breathed into his mouth. He claimed her in a searing kiss. Blood rushed to her head, making her clutch at the lapels on his jacket to keep upright. Burying his hand deep in her hair, he ruined the careful waves as he tilted her head to the perfect angle to ravish her lips. The throb of his erection pressed against her stomach, and she stretched on tiptoe, trying to get it to rub against more interesting places.

"Don't make me fetch a bucket of water, you two." The acerbic tones of Miss Kathy broke them apart. Rory struggled to catch her breath, turning away from Sander's lipstick-smeared mouth before she started to giggle. "You found him, then?" Miss Kathy continued, her dark eyes fixed on Sander.

"I couldn't have done it without your assistance. I want to thank you for speaking to Ryker and Saja for me." Sincerity shone in her mate's eyes, and the older woman waved him off with a grin.

"I get damn tired of this town thinking my nephew is the Bogeyman. I remember when Erik vanished nigh on three years ago. Magnum was madder than a snake by then, taking against anyone and everyone. Ryker did what he could against that damn blood oath, never killed anyone unless expressly ordered to do so." The old woman harrumphed, tossing her silver-black braid over her shoulder. "Come on, girls. Let's show these youngsters how to move."

The matrons returned to the main hall, shooing the remnants of the crowd before them. Sander took Rory by the hand and tugged her after them, but she stayed him with a soft touch on his arm. "What's the matter, honey? I know I'm late but we've still got time for a dance."

All the years she had waited for this moment, to prove to herself and everyone else she was worthy of his attention, and yet somehow it didn't matter one bit. "I want you to hold me in your arms, Sander, but not on the dance floor."

A sexy smile tilted the corner of his mouth as he

scooped her into his arms and turned toward the exit. Rory rested her head against his shoulder, utterly content.

There was, after all, more than one type of mating dance.

About the Author

Merryn Dexter is a military spouse who, after a varied employment career (from selling sandals to old ladies with bunions to being a health and safety coordinator for a construction company), is thrilled to be pursuing her dream career as a romance writer. She likes The Winchesters, Spike, Hotch, Loki and watching complicated European Noir. Her hobbies include crying at books, crying at movies, crying at tv serials (there's a theme!) and believes all stories should have a Happy Ending.

Other Books by Merryn Dexter

A Mate's Healing Touch

A Mate's Redeeming Touch

A Mate's Forgiving Touch

Silver Moon

Soul of Flame

Boss of Me

Renewed Spirits

www.ingramcontent.com/pod-product-compliance
Lightning Source LLC
Chambersburg PA
CBHW060942120626
46557CB00003B/1102